Robert C. Winthrop, William G. McCabe

Virginia Schools Before and After the Revolution

with a sketch of Frederick William Coleman and Lewis Minor Coleman - An

address delivered before the Society of the alumni of the University of

Virginia, June 27th, 1888

Robert C. Winthrop, William G. McCabe

Virginia Schools Before and After the Revolution
with a sketch of Frederick William Coleman and Lewis Minor Coleman - An address delivered before the Society of the alumni of the University of Virginia, June 27th, 1888

ISBN/EAN: 9783337235765

Printed in Europe, USA, Canada, Australia, Japan

Cover: Foto ©Andreas Hilbeck / pixelio.de

More available books at **www.hansebooks.com**

VIRGINIA SCHOOLS

BEFORE AND AFTER THE REVOLUTION,

WITH A SKETCH OF

FREDERICK WILLIAM COLEMAN, M. A.,

AND

LEWIS MINOR COLEMAN, M. A.

AN ADDRESS

DELIVERED BEFORE THE

SOCIETY OF THE ALUMNI

OF THE

UNIVERSITY OF VIRGINIA,

June 27th., 1888,

BY

W. GORDON McCABE,

PETERSBURG, VA.

PUBLISHED BY A STANDING ORDER OF THE SOCIETY.

CHARLOTTESVILLE, VA.:
Chronicle Steam Book and Job Office.
1890.

PREFATORY NOTE.

For valuable information in regard to Frederick William Coleman, my grateful acknowledgements are specially due his life-long friend and class-mate, Colonel Frank G. Ruffin, of Richmond, and his old pupils, Professor Edward S. Joynes, M. A., LL. D. of the University of South Carolina, and Professor Gray Carroll, M. A., of Fauquier; also to Gov. Jno. L. Marye, of Fredericksburg, and Dr. John Roy Baylor, of Caroline, both old "Concord boys."

In preparing the sketch of Lewis Minor Coleman, apart from my personal recollections, I have been greatly indebted for many important details to his widow, Mrs. Mary Ambler Coleman, of Fauquier, and to the Rt. Rev. Thomas U. Dudley, M. A., LL. D., Bishop of Kentucky, long a pupil at "Hanover." Reference has also been made to the admirable sketch of Lewis Coleman by his closest friend, Professor Charles Morris, M. A., published in the *University Memorial.*

Touching the genealogy of the Colemans, my thanks are due to Mrs. Alice Coleman De Jarnette, of Caroline, niece of Frederick W. Coleman, and to George W. Fleming, Esq., of Hanover, half-brother of Lewis M. Coleman.

I desire also to make acknowledgment to my friend, Dr. Bennett W. Green, of Norfolk, and to Mr. Frank Rives Lassiter, of Petersburg, both keen antiquarians, for verifying references to colonial records.

In appending such a volume of notes and number of citations to so slight a contribution to our educational history, I may, perhaps, lay myself open to the imputation of affectation of research and vanity of display. But, after mature deliberation, I have deemed it best to make them. The field of investigation is "virgin soil," and this is far from an exhaustive discussion of this most interesting subject. The scanty information contained in the text has been gleaned from a very considerable number of books. These books, with scarce an exception, have no indexes, and the references I have given may prove suggestive and render no small service hereafter to some one, who may possess the requisite leisure to make a more thorough study of our colonial secondary education. It is almost needless to say that only a portion of the address was delivered.

Mr. President, Gentlemen of the Alumni, Ladies and Gentlemen :

I come to speak to you of two men who deserved well of the State—two men who wrought a great and lasting work in Virginia, yet whose names are to-day but a mere memory to all save kinsmen and friends, and whose services, illustrious as they were, are fast becoming but vague tradition.

I shall speak of them in homely fashion, as befits the theme ; for their lives were in truth so simple, so direct, so veracious, that they disdain, as it were, all efforts at brilliant rhetoric, and check with robust scorn the rippling periods of studied eulogy.

Both of them carried off the highest honors of this University—both of them devoted their great attainments and commanding energies to the furtherance of her fame and of her usefulness—and to both of them belongs in almost equal measure the supreme distinction of having so changed the whole face of secondary education in this Commonwealth, and of having so raised and ennobled the profession to which they consecrated their lives, as henceforth drew to it no mean part of the very flower of our youth.

I come to speak to you of the life and work of Frederick William Coleman, the virtual founder of Concord Academy, and of his nephew and pupil, Lewis Minor Coleman, founder of Hanover Academy—as truly the pioneers of the New Education in our Virginia of the nineteenth century, as were Colet and Erasmus the pioneers of the " New Learning" in the England of the sixteenth.

With a rough impatience, characteristic of the high spirit and imperious nature of the man, the elder broke sharply with every tradition of " the old order" as to methods of instruction and the treatment of boys, while happily for the permanent success of the bold experiment, he was promptly seconded by the courageous efforts of his gentler pupil, who caught up the spirit of the master whom he revered, and, by many wise modifications, developed to full fruition the noble, though crude, ideals of his kinsman.

Working on essentially the same lines as did Arnold of Rugby, when as yet even the name of the great Englishman was unknown to them, they wrought so honestly and fearlessly, with such manly enthusiasm and singleness of purpose, that within a brief space of years they raised, as I have said, the whole tone of secondary education in the State, both as to methods and morals, and so improved the quality of academic instruction, that this University in turn was enabled to advance the standards of the higher education and establish such severe tests of scholarship as would have been manifestly unjust prior to that time.*

Not often is it given to a pioneer to look upon the full fruition of his venture, but happily public opinion in Virginia was ripe for revolt from the old monastic ideas of school discipline. The tiny spark kindled in the neglected "broom-straw" fields of Caroline spread with lightning-like rapidity, and both of these men lived to see, as the fitting crown of their labors, the establishment of schools in every section of the State—in Tidewater and Piedmont, in the Southside and in the Valley—created by sheer force of noble example—informed with the same high spirit as that of "Concord," and fashioned on the same model as that of "Hanover."

And at the very outset, let me say that, apart from the great reforms they established as to methods of instruction, it is difficult to overestimate the debt which the profession of teaching, *as a profession*, owes these men.

*Col. Ruffin dwells on this point in his admirable letter to me in regard to Frederick Coleman's work.

It is idle to tread delicately and use ambiguous phrases. Up to the time that their decisive influence in shaping the lives of young men began to make itself felt as a social power to be taken into account, and the notable results of their chosen work had compelled recognition of the inherent dignity and nobility of their calling, it is but bare truth to say that, save by grudging acquiescence, the teacher, *as a teacher*, rarely " sat above the salt."

If the teacher happened to be a clergyman, he received, of course, the respect due his cloth.

But I am speaking of the teacher pure and simple, and of the social status of his calling in the eyes of the ruling class.

The Virginian, along with his strain of English blood, inherited his full share of what is euphemistically called " English conservatism," and, late into the present century, many a man, who in theory held extreme democratic doctrine as to equality, denied it in practice on more than one social point, and clung with true English tenacity to the traditions of the eighteenth century society. Exceptions there were, of course, even outside the clergy, as we shall presently see in the case of the progenitors of the Colemans, but, as a rule, the schoolmaster was looked upon by the Virginia gentry with a feeling somewhat akin to that with which the private tutor and domestic chaplain was regarded in the great houses in the days of "good Queen Anne"—when he was held a sort of upper menial, who humbly withdrew from the table after the first course, unless my lord was in his cups, and, calling another bottle, bade him remain as the butt of his tipsy satire, or my lady was graciously pleased to challenge him to a game of tric-trac to while away the long, dull winter evenings.

And to speak truth, there had been much in the character of the early Virginia school-masters—much in the character of many of their successors in the present century—to justify this feeling of contempt for their calling.

Pardon my dwelling for a space on the deplorable lack of educational advantages in Virginia, not only throughout the whole colonial period, but for many years after the Revolution.

Mr. Cabott Lodge, in his "*History of the English Colonies in America*," tells us that "there is no indication in the statutes of any desire in Virginia to provide education." This is by no means true, as a careful reading of Hening* abundantly proves, but it is true, unfortunately, that these educational enactments were allowed to slumber quietly in the statute-book.

Unquestionably, there was no *system* of elementary or secondary education in the colony, nor is the reason far to seek.

In his recent monograph on "*William and Mary College*," Dr. Herbert Adams, of the Johns Hopkins University, says :

"Virginia was a new country, extraordinarily attractive from an agricultural point of view. Her settlers, instead of gathering in towns and villages, as the settlers of New England were *by law* required to do, dispersed more and more, imitating the English model of rural society already established by representative Virginians. It might well be expected that it would take a much longer time to develop an educational system in colonial Virginia than in Massachusetts or Connecticut, which were both made up of compact village republics. It took the University of Michigan nearly fifty years to get fairly underway even with the aid of a national land grant, good territorial legislation and the progressive spirit of the great West, of the nineteenth century. The Virginians were well enough disposed towards schools and colleges, but circumstances,

*History of the Eng. Colonies in America, p. 74; but see Hening, II, 25, 30, 37. Foote's Sketches of Virginia, p. 39.

such as physical geography and political economy, were against them."*

Sir William Berkeley, in 1671, in reply to thê Lords Commissioners of Foreign Plantations, touching the progress of learning in the colony, said : " I thank God there are no free schools nor printing, and I hope we shall not have these hundred years ; for learning has brought disobedience and heresy and sects into the world, and printing has divulged them and libels against the best government ; God keep us from them both."†

Substantially Berkeley's hope was realized.

True, owing to the energy and courageous persistency of James Blair, " William and Mary" was chartered in 1692 and firmly established. But that was all.

All the Stuart governors of the colony were hostile to general education, and how influential men in the mother-

---

*Adams's College of William and Mary, p. 14.

†Hening II, 511–517. Patrick Copeland, chaplain in the service of the East India Company, was the projector of the first English free school in North America, a building for which was commenced at Charles City, and in 1622 was also elected President of the College at Henrico. Owing to the Indian troubles he never came to Virginia. In 1625 he went out to Bermudas, at a salary of 100 marks as minister, and to have "a free school erected for the bringing up of youths in literature and good learning." In 1626 the Bermudas Council was urged to support the free school. The governor, in writing to London touching the matter, growls, as Berkeley did nearly fifty years later, " I wish we had ministers contented to preach the gospel and let this free school alone until we are free of debt." See Neill's *Virginia Carolorum*, pp. 196, 197. See *Foote*, p. 11.

Dr. Adams (*William and Mary*, p. 13) says, in regard to Berkeley's crusty utterance : " The times were not yet ripe for classical education in Virginia, for this was what the term 'free school' meant in the seventeenth century. It was free in the sense of teaching the liberal arts, preparatory to college training. In old England and in her colonies, free schools were originally synonymous with Latin schools or grammar schools. It would be as absurd to identify the ancient and modern meanings of free schools as to confuse a modern grammar school with the earlier or classical use of that term." It is with great diffidence that I dissent from the opinion of such an accomplished scholar as Dr. Adams, but I must do so in regard to the meaning of the term in colonial Virginia. See *Virginia Carolorum*, pp.

country regarded the plea of Virginia for help in fostering
learning, may be inferred from the amiable reply of Sey-
mour, the attorney general, when Blair was pressing for
the issue of the charter authorized by the king and queen.
As the chief reason for planting the college, Blair urged
the necessity of a proper training school for ministers of
the gospel,. modestly alleging that Virginians had souls to
be saved as well as Englishmen.

"Souls!" cries Mr. Attorney General, "Damn your
souls! Make tobacco!"*

Fifty years after Berkeley's crusty utterance the Bishop
(in 1723) of London addressed a circular to the clergy of
Virginia, then somewhat over forty in number, making
various inquiries as to the condition of things in the parishes. One of the questions was : "Are there any schools
in your parish?" The answer, with two or three exceptions, (and those in favor of charity schools,) was, "None."
Another question was, "Is there any parish library?"
The answer invariably was, "None," except in one case,
where the minister replied, "We have the Book of Homilies, the Whole Duty of Man, and the Singing Psalms."†

Throughout the whole colonial period, such secondary
education as existed was almost entirely in the hands of

113, 197. *Meade*, I, 265. *Hening*, VII, p. 41. Jones's *Present State of Virginia*, p. 84. Through the courtesy of Franklin B. Dexter, Esq., Librarian
of Yale University, I am also enabled to cite the following passage from
the "New Haven Records," as indicating the meaning of "free school"
in colonial New England in the seventeenth century : "The 25th of 12th
mon[th], 1641...... Itt is ordered that a free schoole shall be sett up in
this towne and our pastor, Mr. Davenport, together with the magistrates,
shall consider whatt yearly allowance is meete to be given to itt out of
the como stock of the towne, and allso whatt rules and orders are meete
to be observed in and about the same."

Foote, p. 152. *Historical Sketch of William and Mary* (Morrison), p. 33.

†Meade's Old Churches and Old Families of Virginia, I, page 190 ; but
Hugh Jones in his *Present State of Virginia* (1724), says : "In most Parishes
are Schools (little houses being built on Purpose) where are taught *English*
and *Writing*; but to prevent the sowing the Seeds of Dissension and

the "parsons," who on their glebes, or, if unmarried, at the houses of the great land owners, conducted what were long known as the "*Parsons' Schools.*"*

It is not a pleasant thing for a Virginian and an Episcopalian to say, but a more disreputable class of men than the early Virginia parsons, it would be difficult to imagine.

They diced, rode to hounds, backed their favorite birds at the county cocking-mains, could call a bottle as gallantly as any roaring young squire, and, like His Reverence Parson Sampson, in Thackeray's *Virginians*, were quite ready, when they came down out of the pulpit on Sunday, to give or take odds against the favorite in the great "Four-Year-Old Sweepstakes," to be run presently at Williamsburg.

The cold and worldly spirit which pervaded the Church of England at the time in the mother-country, was only too faithfully reflected in the Colonial Establishment, and such contemporary memoirs as have come down to us leave little room to doubt that our Virginia parsons, instead of setting a pious and godly example to their spiritual cures, but too often aped the manners and habits of the most dissolute of the laity, and were as subservient to the great land-owners† as any rural vicar in England to the lord of the manor.

Well-authenticated tradition has, however, handed down an amusing instance of a doughty parson in Tidewater, who was anything but subservient.

He and his vestry quarreled, and the vestries, you must remember, were a great social and political power in those

Faction, it is to be wished that the Masters or Mistresses should be such as are approved or licensed by the Minister and Vestry of the Parishes, or Justices of the County ; the Clerks of the Parishes being generally most proper for this Purpose ; or, (in Case of their Incapacity or Refusal) such others as can best be procured." (Page 70.)

*Meade I, p. 190.

†Jones's *Present State of Virginia*, p. 104. *Meade* I, p. 191.

days, being composed almost exclusively of the ruling class*—from words they came to blows—and the parson, who was a man of notable physical strength, not only thrashed single-handed the whole opposing array, but added a deeper pang to the bitterness of defeat by justifying his conduct in a sermon on the next Sabbath from the text in Nehemiah : " *And I contended with them, and cursed them, and smote certain of them, and plucked off their hair.*"†

Do not misunderstand me.

Assuredly, among these early Virginia parsons, in whose hands was the secondary education, there were not a few men of godly walk and sound scholarship. Especially is this true of the clergy of the seventeenth century. But in the eighteenth century they steadily declined in character, and the great majority of them were, as good old Bishop Meade sorrowfully says, men of "most evil living."‡

Of those who conducted excellent schools early in the eighteenth century, may be mentioned the Rev. Archibald Campbell, who long taught a famous school in the county of Westmoreland, which, according to tradition, counted among its pupils John Marshall and James Monroe.‖ The Rev. Thomas Martin,§ also master of a school in this "Athens of America," as Westmoreland was proudly called in those early days, who prepared James Madison for Princeton College ; and, notably, the Rev. James Maury, of Orange,¶ an elegant scholar and zealous teacher, who

---

*Meade I, p. 151.

†Meade I, p. 18.

‡Meade I, pp. 16, 163, *pass.* *Foote*, pp. 34, 310. *Westover Mss.* I, p. 7. *Life of Rev. Devereux Jarratt, passim.* But see too *Foote*, p. 149.

‖See *Meade* I, p. 159.

§See Rives' *Life of Madison*, vol. 1. *Princeton College During the Eighteenth Century*, p. 78.

¶The plaintiff in the celebrated " Parson's Cause," in which Patrick Henwas the preceptor of many eminent Virginians, chief of them, Thomas Jefferson, who remained his lifelong friend.

In these *Parsons' Schools*, Latin and Greek, according to the fashion of the time in England, were the chief subjects taught. But instruction was given in Algebra, Euclid and Land Surveying, and we find French and Spanish also taught in the once celebrated school conducted by an erudite Scotch "Dominie," Donald Robertson,* whom Madison long afterwards, when Secretary of State, gratefully remembered as his first preceptor, and termed "the learned teacher of King and Queen county, Virginia."

But according to the old-fashioned ideas, the strong point of the *Parsons' Schools* was the discipline. As Thackeray says, in describing that famous scene, when that resolute little woman, "Madame Esmond," ordered the Rev. Mr. Ward to administer a flogging to that high-strung young "Virginian," George Warrington, "the *baculine* method was quite a common mode of argument in those days," and lads of mischievous spirit made light of being "horsed," as the phrase then was, by pedagogues, whom they yet looked down upon as their inferiors.

Speaking of a once famous schoolmaster, Parson O'Neil, who taught in your neighboring county of Orange, Bishop Meade† describes with sympathetic gusto his methods of inculcating obedience :

---

ry, representing the defendants, first made himself famous by his treasonable utterances against the King, which practically won the case for his clients "despite the law and the evidence."—*Wirt's Life of Patrick Henry*. James Maury had a flourishing school at the foot of Peters' Mountain, in Orange county. His son, Rev. Walker Maury, succeeded him, and afterwards moved the school to Williamsburg, (as we shall see further on), where he conducted the most successful academy in the South. Another son, Matthew, was also a teacher and clergyman. *Meade* II, p. 44.

. *See Rives' *Life of Madison*, vol. I.

†*Meade* II, p. 90, Parson O'Neil, we are told, was "more a teacher than a preacher." Another "Dominie," noted for his unsparing use of the rod, was the Rev. John Cameron, D. D., a graduate of King's College, Aber-

" Flogging," says the worthy Bishop, "was a main in-
gredient in the practice of his system. He had a summary
method of reducing and gentling a refractory youth.
Mounting him upon the back of an athletic negro man,
whom he seems to have kept for the purpose, the culprit
was pinioned hand and foot as in a vice, and, with the unsparing application of the rod to his defenceless back, was
taught the lesson, if not the doctrine, of passive obedience."

I may add that there are many men yet living, who
preserve a smarting remembrance that the good Bishop
himself, who taught school for many years before his elevation to the Episcopate, wielded with lusty arm what
Shakspere calls "the threatening twigs of birch," and
ever possessed a most robust faith in the efficacy of that
remedy which King Solomon prescribed as a certain pre-
ventive against the spoiling of children.

Touching elementary instruction in the colony, Sir William Berkeley declared that the people of Virginia followed
"the same course that is taken in England out of towns ;
every man according to his ability instructing his children." "We have forty-eight parishes," growls His Excellency, "and our ministers are well paid, and, by my
consent, should be better, *if they would pray oftener and
preach less*."*

*The first legacy by a resident of the American plantations
of England for the promotion of free education was given
by Benjamin Symmes, of Virginia*. This was in 1634,
four years before John Harvard, a non-conforming clergyman of England, who had been resident in the colony of
Massachusetts but a single year, bequeathed the half of
his estate and his entire library to the college, which now

deen, who came over to Virginia from Scotland in 1770, and long taught a
select classical school in Lunenburg county, where he was also minister of
the parish.

*Hening, II, 511 *sqq.*   Foote, p. 34.

bears his name. Symmes, by his will, made Feb'y 12th, 1634-'5, gave two hundred acres of land on the Poquoson River, which flows into Chesapeake Bay, "together with the milk and increase of eight cows for the maintenance of a learned and honest man to keep upon the said ground a free school, for the education and instruction of the children of the adjoining parishes of Elizabeth City and Kiquotan, from Mary's Mount downward to the Poquoson River."*

The example of this first American benefactor to the cause of free education was not without results in his section of the colony, for we find that forty years later, in 1675, worthy Master Henry Peasley "doth devise six hundred acres of land lying in the parish of Abingdon, County of Gloucester, together with ten cows and one breeding mare, for the maintenance of a free schoole forever, to be kept with a schoole master for the education of the children of the parishes of Abingdon and Ware forever."

The former of these bequests seems to have been fruitful of results, but little or nothing came of the latter, for seventy-five years after the devise, we find in Hening† an act appointing trustees for the care of the property, wherein is recited that up to that time (1756), scarcely anything had been done to carry out the charitable intention of the donor.

More fortunate was the bequest of Samuel Sandford of London—"some time of Accomack county, Virginia"—who in 1710 "for the benefit, better learning and education of poor children, whose parents are esteemed unable to give them learning, living in the upper part of Accomack county in Virginia," devised the rents and profits of three

---

* *Virginia Carolorum*, p. 113. *Hening*, I, 252. *Campbell's Hist. Va.*, p. 209.

† *Hening*, VII, 41. See *Meade*, I, p. 329.

thousand four hundred and twenty acres of land, "humbly praying the Honourable, the Governor of Virginia, for the time being, with the Honourable Council of State, their care that the lands by this will given may be appropriated for the uses intended and prescribed."* This school flourished for many years.

Occasionally such of the white "apprentices" on the plantations as discovered an aptitude for books, were given the privilege of attending with their "betters" the *Parsons' Schools*, and some of these, in turn, taught, what were known far into the present century as, " *Old Field Schools*," which the sons of the gentry were sometimes forced to attend for lack of better.

Washington's first school, in the county of Stafford, was an "Old Field School," taught by one of his father's tenants, named Hobby, who was also sexton of the parish.†

His brother, Lawrence, in accordance with the prevailing fashion of the times for the eldest son, was sent at the age of fifteen to England to receive "a gentleman's education."

In these schools were taught only "the three royal R's," and of how slender was the equipment of the masters, we can form some notion from the autobiographical letters of the Rev. Devereux Jarratt, who tells us with manly simplicity that he did not belong to the class of "gentle folks"; that he attended one of these *Old ·Field Schools* for several years ; learned the trade of a carpenter while still a lad ; wearied of it ; and at the age of nineteen was induced to become a teacher, notwithstanding his meagre preparation. For several years he taught what he calls "a plain school" in Fluvanna—then a part of Albemarle—

---

*From the county records of Accomac, quoted by *Meade*, I. p. 265.

†*Irving's Life of Washington*, I. p. 20. "A convict servant whom his father bought for a schoolmaster," according to Rev. Jonathan Boucher. See M. D. Conway's *Washington and Mt. Vernon*, p. xxix.

at an annual salary of nine pounds, seven shillings, current Virginia money.*

It is pleasant to add that this pious and godly man so improved himself while teaching, that at the age of thirty, having gone to England for his ordination, he is said to have passed the most creditable examination of all the candidates presented to the Bishop of London, though the majority of the "postulants" were graduates of Oxford and Cambridge. He returned to Virginia in 1763, was an ardent patriot in the Revolution, and down to the close of the last century was famous both as a preacher and school-master.

Yet, despite the lack of good schools, elementary and secondary, for the great mass of the colonists, there were, unquestionably, many highly-educated men in the province, of whom William Byrd, of Westover, and Lewis Burwell,† of "King's Mill," stand out as conspicuous types. The polished oratory of Richard Henry Lee was applauded to the echo by his fellow Burgesses, who took the keenest delight in his frequent classical allusions and in the exquisite symmetry of his sonorous periods.

The truth seems to be, that while the poor, as we have seen, had few or no educational opportunities, the ruling class, numerically small, was from the earliest days keenly alive to the importance of securing thorough education for their children.

In the great families, there was not only the parson-tutor, but we find the elementary instruction carefully looked after by the mothers.

Such records as have come down to us, afford conclu-

*It is interesting to note the cost of tuition in these country schools in the middle of the 18th century. Mr. Jarratt says: "I now (1752) got a school of twelve or thirteen scholars at 20s. per scholar, which was the usual price in those days," *Life of Rev. Devereux Jarratt,* edited by the Rev. James Coleman, p. 38.

†*Cooke's Virginia,* p. 407.

sive proof that, in most instances, they were well-equipped
for the task. Many of them, as even the idlest reader knows,
were women of vigorous common sense, of great decision
of character, accustomed to exact obedience and reverence, even when their children had grown to manhood and
womanhood, and withal added to the native Virginia
mother-wit no mean acquirement. Some of them had
been trained by their fathers, who, educated in humane
letters in the mother-country, held it a paramount duty to
devote a large share of their abundant leisure to the personal supervision of the education of both sons and
daughters.*

Exquisitely did these Virginia mothers teach the little
ones the now "lost art of reading," and patiently did they
ground them in the elements of Latin and in English.

They knew not a few of the best English authors, not,
as so many of their fair descendants do, from "hand-
books," but from the pages of the authors themselves.

The libraries were small—Shakspere, Dryden, Tillot-
son's Sermons, Montaigne in translation, "The Spectator,"
Pope, and a few others—but these they knew almost by
heart, and the letters of many of them, still extant,† display a command of vigorous and graceful English, which
the cleverest Vassar graduate must regard with envy.

Blessed with a large staff of thoroughly trained ser-
vants (for your native Virginian always avoided speaking
of these faithful family dependants as "slaves"), they were
not only notable housewives, but took the time to instruct
their children soundly in morals and in the rudiments of a
liberal education.

As the boys grew older, if there was no family tutor,

---

*See *Memoirs of a Huguenot Family*, p. 366. Numberless citations could
be given from Meade and others.

†Cf. especially the letters of Mrs. Anne Nicholas (daughter of Col. Wilson Cary, of Hampton), Mrs. Matthew Maury (Mary Ann Fontaine), and
Mrs. Edward Carrington, (Eliza Ambler).

they rode off resplendent in lace ruffles, silver shoe-buckles and bravely-laced hat, followed at a respectful distance by " Gumbo," to attend some Parson's school in the neighboring parish, there to be ~~only~~ prepared for William and Mary.

But many of the anxious mothers were afraid to expose their darlings to the temptations of the gay little capital, and the freedom from discipline enjoyed by " the gilded youth" of that ancient foundation, who tempered the dreary tasks of the Eton and Westminster grammars by " keeping race-horses at ye college and betting at ye billiard and other gaming tables "—venial peccadilloes, in which they but followed the example of their reverend instructors.*

Thus, many of them were sent to England to be edu-

---

*See extracts from proceedings of the Faculty, Sept. ye 14th, 1752, quoted in the *Hist. Sketch of the College of William and Mary* (Morrison), p. 42. *Meade*, I, 175 sq. Doyle's *English Colonies in America*, I, p. 274. In the curious pamphlet entitled *A Modest Answer to a Malicious Libel Against His Excellency, Francis Nicholson*, may be found an acconnt of a "barring-out" escapade on the part of the young collegians. As regards *William and Mary* (in the earlier years of the 18th century at least), the dispassionate student of contemporaneous documents, must find much to justify Doyle's assertion that " it was nothing better than a boarding-school, in which Blair had no small difficulty in contending against the extravagance and license engendered by the home-training of his pupils." But he adds, " There was no lack of mental culture in Virginia. While the accomplished and highly-trained country gentlemen of the seventeenth century, the Elliot or Hampden, had gradually degenerated into the Sir Roger or Squire Western of the eighteenth, the Virginia planter had risen in the scale. But the young colonist was either taught by a tutor, who was often also the domestic chaplain of the plantation, or was sent for education to one of the Northern colonies or to the mother country"—I, 274. Very few, if any, went to the " Northern colonies." No Virginians went to Harvard or Yale prior to the Revolution, and very few to Princeton. But numbers went to " the mother-country." See *Meade*, I, pp. 190, 192. There seems little doubt that *among the ruling class* there was a broader and deeper culture in Virginia in the 17th and the early years of 18th centuries than in any of the other colonies, save possibly Massachusetts.

cated at Eton and other famous schools, passing thence to
the universities, or, perhaps, if they showed no further
concern for humane letters, being allowed a season in
"town," to learn from the beaux of Soho and St. James
"the nice conduct of a clouded cane" and other elegances
of fashion, wherewith to dazzle the colonial beauties on
their return. The Lees, the Randolphs, the Nelsons, and
many others, whose names are famous in Virginia annals,
were so educated even up to the time of the Revolution,*
and came back as highly trained as any of their English
cousins of the time.

But the young Virginian who ran across the sea for the
higher education, simply changed his sky and not his

---

*The strong individuality of the Virginia planters is shown in their in-
dependence of each other in the selection of schools in the mother-country for their children. The Pages went to Eton, the Meades to Harrow,
the Corbins to Winchester, the Lees, Beverleys, Bollings, Munfords, Fair-
faxes and Blands to Leeds Academy in Yorkshire. The choice as to the
universities was naturally influenced by the preferences of the masters of
the schools to which the young Virginians were sent. But this was not
always the case. The Rev. Chris. Atkinson, head-master of the Leeds
Academy, urged that young Theodorick Bland should be sent to Oxford,
but he and his father decided for Edinburgh. There were so many Virginians attending the medical lectures at the latter University, that they
formed a "Virginia Club" (1761), one of the first "articles" of which prescribed that "every constituent of this club shall be a Virginian born."
The club was established "for the improvement of its members in anat-
omy." "Physick" was not in the earliest days of the colony considered
a fit profession for a gentleman. Theodorick Bland "was among the first
persons in Virginia that devoted themselves to the study of medicine."
See Campbell's Memoir prefixed to the *Bland Papers*, p. xv, sq. and p. xix.
As a rule, the young Virginian, who went to England to study, went to get
"a polite education" and not to prepare himself for a profession. Some
like Wm. Byrd of Westover (a graduate of Oxford), John Ambler of
Jamestown (graduate of Cambridge), and John Banister of Battersea, studied at "the Temple," but they were all young men of ample fortune, and
had no need to practice the law. Others, however, (e. g., John Blair and
Sir John Randolph), practiced law on their return to the colony, in which
many young men of the aristocratic class were members of the colonial
bar. See Wynne's Notes to *A Memoir of a Portion of the Bolling Family
in England and America*, pp. 33, 34 and 37 sqq.

mind, and never hesitated a moment as to where his allegiance lay, when the foolish policy of Lord North denied the chartered liberties of the Old Dominion.

He had been reared to reverence Church and King, but he was as jealous as any Englishman born of his rights as a freeman of Anglo-Saxon blood.

He was deeply attached to the "tiny mother-isle," which his father, settled on the banks of the York or the James, ever fondly spoke of as "home," but there was bred in his bone a still deeper devotion to the principles which, since the days of Runnymede, had been the common heritage of all English-speaking folk.

And it is a proud memory for the descendants of these young patricians, that, when the dun war-cloud lowered in the West, and Virginia was driven to choose between submission and resistance, to a man they doffed academic cap and gown, and turning their backs on the grey cloisters of Winchester and Eton, came trooping home to offer their swords to the new nation—just as nearly a hundred years after, when the rights of Virginia were in jeopardy and her soil about to be invaded, her sons, yonder at Berlin and Leipzig, at Göttingen and the schools of the Sorbonne, tossed aside their books and came swarming back to defend under her proud *Sic Semper* the heritage bequeathed them by their fathers.

As Marshal Ney said, when he saw the beardless young conscripts rushing in all the joyous valor of youth upon the Russian guns at Weissenfels, " *C'est dans le sang !* *C'est dans le sang !*"—"It's in the blood ! It's in the blood !"

Beverley in his *History and Present State of Virginia*, published in 1705, tells us[*] that there were at that time "very few Dissenters" in the province, but before the middle of the century we find them in every part of the

---

[*]Bk. IV, Part I, Ch. 7, p. 210.

colony—the Baptists in Fluvanna and Spottsylvania, on the sea-coast and in the Valley—the German Tunkers and Mennonites in the lower Valley along the Opequon, under the shadow of soaring Massinnutton—the Quakers in Nansemond and elsewhere—the German Lutherans in Madison, along the Rappahannock—above all, the sturdy Scotch-Irish Presbyterians, some from Pennsylvania and New Jersey, where they had tarried for a time with their kinsmen, until assured of protection for their religion, under the Toleration Act of William and Mary, by His Excellency, Governor Gooch, they swarmed southwards to take up the rich lands of the smiling Valley of the Shenandoah—others direct from across the seas, driven from Ulster by English persecution and led by John Lewis, father of that Andrew Lewis, who, in fringed hunting-shirt, rifle in hand, looks down upon us in "counterfeit presentment" of enduring bronze from his pedestal yonder in Richmond—the perfect type of that glorious stock, which for many a year held the border of our "Antient Dominion" against wild foray of Shawnee and Cherokee—that dauntless race, in whose breast "beat so strong the fear of God, that there was left no room for fear of any other thing," and who, ever counting life itself a worthless thing when freedom is at stake, gave Andrew Lewis to the first Revolution and Stonewall Jackson to the second.*

Other Presbyterian settlements there were—in the lower Valley from the Potomac to Winchester—in Charlotte and Prince Edward—notably that in Hanover, where sundry heads of families revolting from the worldly preaching and practices of the Establishment, knew not at first what to call themselves,† but finally became the very centre of Presbyterian faith and influence.

---

*Cooke's Virginia, p. 326.

†For a most interesting account of this secession from the Established Church, see Foote, p. 121 sqq.

Of all the Dissenters, the Presbyterians were the first in point of wealth, character and position ; and, as we might naturally expect, the question of providing a sound education for their children early claimed their attention.

In 1747, Samuel Davies,* afterwards President of Princeton College, and virtual founder of the Presbyterian church in Virginia, came as an evangelist to Hanover county. He had been educated at the famous classical school of Samuel Blair at Fogg's Manor in Pennsylvania. He was a young man of engaging manners, reputed a profound theologian, a keen debater, as Attorney-General Peyton Randolph afterwards found to his cost,† liberal in his feelings towards the Establishment, and withal endowed with such wondrous powers of eloquence, that Patrick Henry declared him "the greatest orator he had ever heard."

Davies himself was never master of a school,‡ but it was owing to his persistent efforts that Virginia owed the first classical schools taught by men outside the communion of the Established Church.

The masters were in nearly every instance graduates of Princeton, with here and there an assistant from the "log-colleges" of Pennsylvania. Thus, we find, between 1750 and 1760, a good classical school in Louisa, under the mastership of the Rev. John Todd,‖ of the class of 1747, who had as assistant the Rev. James Waddell, reputed one of the best Latinists of his day, afterwards famous as "the Blind Preacher," whose eloquence William Wirt declares in "*The British Spy*" was beyond that of Massillon or Bourdaloue.§

Foote, Ch. X.

†The story is told at length in *Foote*, p. 293.

‡" Mr. Davies promoted classical schools, though his multiplied labors prevented his being the head of one in Virginia." *Foote*, p. 221.

‖*Princeton Coll. in 18th Cent.*, p. 7.

§*Foote*. p. 381, *sqq.*

Other teachers from Princeton later on were, Hezekiah Balch,* of the class of 1766, who taught a classical school in Fauquier, migrating after the Revolution to Tennessee, where his strenuous efforts gave an impulse to education throughout the whole Southwestern region ; and Daniel McCalla,† of the same class, who established an academy in Hanover, which he seems to have given up after the Revolution by reason of being "eminently social" and "not always discreet."

It will be observed that the old Parsons were not alone in their lapses from strict sobriety, for we find in the early years of the Revolution, Mr. John Springer, also a Princeton graduate, calling together the Board of Trustees of Hampden Sidney Academy to confess that "he had been drunk and did gamble at New London on one occasion,"‡ "in consideration of which candor the Trustees only suspended him." As might be expected of so honest a youth, he afterwards became one of the godliest men in the Presbyterian ministry.

But the chief schools founded under the auspices of Hanover Presbytery were the "Augusta Academy," the germ of the present Washington and Lee University, and the "Prince Edward Academy," the germ of Hampden Sidney College.‖

In 1771, we find the Presbytery, on motion of the Rev. Samuel Stanhope Smith, discussing the subject of education, but it was not until three years later, in 1774, that William Graham, a class-mate at Princeton of "Light Horse Harry Lee," and reputed a young man of notable

---

*Princeton Coll. in 18th Cent., p. 104.

†Ib. p. 109.

‡Foote, p. 401.

‖The statements in the text touching "Augusta Academy" (afterwards "Liberty Hall") and Hampden Sidney are based on Foote's valuable Sketches of Virginia, Series I.

scholarship, was invited to engage in a classical school in Augusta under the direction of the Rev. John Brown, who had been for some years conducting a small "grammar school" near Mount Pleasant.*

In the same year (1774), Presbytery, taking into consideration (I quote their language) "the great extent of the colony, judge that a public school for the liberal education of youth would be of great importance on the south-side of the Blue Ridge, notwithstanding the appointment of one already made in the county of Augusta, and having been favored with the company of Mr. Samuel Smith, a probationer of New Castle Presbytery in Pennsylvania, a gentleman who has taught the languages for a considerable time in the New Jersey College with good approbation, and with pleasure finding that, if properly encouraged, he may be induced to take charge of such a seminary, we therefore judge it expedient to recommend it to the congregations of Cumberland, Prince Edward, and Brierly in particular, and to all others in general, to set a subscription on foot to purchase a library, philosophical apparatus, and such other things as may be necessary for said purpose."†

The subscriptions poured in rapidly, Samuel Stanhope Smith was chosen Rector, with a staff of assistants, all Princeton men, and in January, 1776, the "Prince Edward Academy" was opened.

The strong point of both Graham and Smith seems, as might be expected from their training, to have been Mental and Moral Philosophy and Belles Lettres.‡ From hints dropped here and there in various books, one may doubt whether in the ancient languages they were the equals of the old Parsons, who, although they had never

---

*See also (in addition to Foote) *Prin. Coll. in 18th Cent.*, p. 163.

†Quoted by *Foote*, p. 393 sq.

‡See *Life of Rev. Archibald Alexander* (ed. 1857), p. 18. *Foote*, p. 461.

heard of logaoedic rhythms or "the classification of the conditional sentence," could read Homer and Demosthenes without a dictionary and quote Horace with an apt felicity, which seems to have gone out with the last century. Stanhope Smith remained but three years at the " Prince Edward Academy," having been called in 1779 to the chair of Moral Philosophy in Princeton.

He was succeeded by his brother, John Blair Smith,* a man of undoubted force of character, who seems to have had the courage of his convictions in things small as well as great, throwing down the gauntlet to Patrick Henry in debate before the Virginia Assembly on the General Assessment Bill, and, with still greater fearlessness, even daring to part his hair in the middle.

The discipline in both these academies, as well as in " Washington Henry Academy," founded a few years after in Hanover under the mastership of John Duburrow Blair,† of the Princeton class of 1775, was, of course, "baculine," and we are told that Graham, a slight, wiry man of middle stature, active as a catamount, would without a moment's hesitation "horse" the most strapping young backwoodsman who dared defy his authority.

The course of study was in the main that pursued at Princeton, and fortunately one of Graham's old pupils has recorded the latter's method of hearing recitations, which was probably that of his brother-teachers. In the *Southern Literary Messenger* for June 1838, there is an article on Graham's school, signed "Senex," who has been identified as the venerable Doctor Campbell of Lexington.

Dr. Campbell visited the school as a lad in 1775, before entering as a pupil, and thus describes the scene :

"I happened at Mt. Pleasant during Mr. Graham's superintendence. It was near the hour of recreation.

Foote, ch, XIX, and *Prin. Coll. in 18th Cent.*, p. 170.

†*Prin. Coll. in 18th Cent.*, p. 182.

Here was seen a large assemblage of fine, vigorous-looking youth, apparently from ten to twenty years of age. They were mostly engaged in feats of strength, speed or agility, each emulous to surpass his fellows in those exercises for which youth of their age generally possess a strong predilection. Presently the sound of a horn summoned all to the business of the afternoon. The sports were dropped as if by magic. Now you may see them seated singly or in pairs, or in small groups, with book in hand, conning over their afternoon's lesson. One portion resorted immediately to the hall, and, ranging themselves before the preceptor in semi-circular order, handed him an open book containing the recitations. He seemed not to look into the book, and presently closed it, thinking, as I supposed, he knew as well as the book. *Of the recitations I understood not a syllable*, yet it was highly agreeable to the ear, sonorous and musical ; and although more than sixty winters have rolled away since that time, the impressions then made have not been entirely effaced from my memory. I have since discovered that the recitation was a portion of that beautiful Greek verb, *Tupto*, in which the sound of the consonants, *pi, tau, mu, theta*, predominate. *It was observable that during the recitation the preceptor gave no instructions, corrected no errors, made no remarks of any kind.* He seemed to sit merely as a silent witness of the performance. *The class itself resembled one of those self-regulating machines of which I have heard.* Each member stood ready, by trapping and turning down, to correct the mishaps and mistakes of his fellows ; and as much emulation was discovered here as had been an hour before on the theatre of their sports in their athletic exercises. During this recitation, an incipient smile of approbation was more than once observed on the countenance of the Preceptor, maugre his native gravity and reserve. This happened when small boys, by their superior scholarship, raised themselves above those who were full grown. This class having gone through, several others, in regular order, presented themselves before the teacher and passed the ordeal. The business of the afternoon was closed by a devotional exercise."*

Such was the method of teaching then in vogue, and I have quoted this passage from Dr. Campbell's article describing the old machine system,† which developed the memory at the expense of the understanding, that you may contrast it with the vitalizing methods introduced by Frederick Coleman, which breathed the breath of life into the dry-bones of the dead languages, which taught a lad first of all to *think*, and, developing in healthy fashion his mental faculties, enabled him not only to read and mark, but inwardly to digest, the highest thought of the great masters of the ancient world.

I may pause a moment to remark that probably no mortal man before or since the time of Dr. Campbell, has ever spoken of *Tupto* as "that beautiful Greek verb." His delight in it, notwithstanding the drawback that he "understood not a syllable," certainly reminds one of the pious old lady, who confessed that she didn't understand much of the sermon, but insisted that she had been "greatly comforted by that blessed word, Mesopotamia."

Then broke the storm of war.

---

*Dr. Archibald Alexander complains of the great paucity of schools in "the Valley," when he was a boy (just before the Revolution), and the character of some of the masters may be judged from that of his first teacher, one John Reardon, like "Hobby," an English convict, whom his father bought at auction in Baltimore, during a business trip to that town. Reardon had been to a classical school (he averred) in London, and had "read in Latin as far as Virgil" and in Greek "a little of the Greek Testament." "The master, as being my father's servant, lodged at our house and often carried me in his arms part of the way (to school). I had no fear of him, as at home I was accustomed to call him Jack, and often conveyed my father's commands to him." *Life*, p. 12.

†*Ib.* p. 13.

Our experience in Virginia during the Civil War en-
ables us to form an intelligent idea of the degree to which
letters were silent amid the clash of arms.

The burning defiance of Patrick Henry had kindled the
flame of patriotism in the breasts of young and old, and
his impassioned utterances found ready echo in the hearts
of gentle and simple alike.

For the time all religious differences and social antago-
nisms were forgotten, and the fires of Revolution were to
weld into a compact mass of resistance the composite elements of Virginia society.

The Churchmen of Tidewater and Piedmont, as of
right, took the lead in the great revolt, and their figures
shine out the noblest and grandest in the broad light of
that heroic time.

But Baptists and Presbyterians followed with glad alac-
rity, for to them Revolution meant not only civil, but
absolute religious, liberty, and from Accomac on the Chesapeake to the furthest outposts on the Alleghanies, the
Dissenting ministers were thundering from their rude pul-
pits that "Rebellion to Tyrants was obedience to God."

The lads of '76, like the lads of '61, were eager to prove
that Valor counted manhood, not by years, but by deeds of
daring, and even in that age of implicit filial obedience,
many were deaf to the remonstrances of parents and
guardians. More than half of the young scions of the
ruling class at William and Mary threw aside their books
with true Cavalier impatience, and exchanging gown for
sword, as did also three of their professors, sought the
headquarters of the Continental army. "Augusta Academy" became "Liberty Hall Academy," and Graham
found his young Scotch-Irish mastiffs straining at the
leash. He himself preached the duty of volunteering,
and, practicing what he preached, was elected Captain of
the Rockbridge contingent under the call of '78. Though

his company was not called into active service, his patri-
otic spirit in the darkest days everywhere infused courage
into doubting hearts, and in 1781, when Tarleton and his
marauding troopers were reported advancing on Staunton
to capture the Virginia Assembly, Graham hearing the
news while on his way to the old Stone Meeting House,
wheels his horse instantly, and, spurring hotly back along
the North Mountain road, rouses the men of Rockbridge
and Augusta, and hurries with them "to the front" to
hold Rockfish Gap.

A thin, silent, dark-browed man, sarcastic of speech,
and "a good hater"; but, let it never be forgotten, a zealous teacher and a dauntless patriot.

"Prince Edward Academy," too, has received the sig-
nificant name of "Hampden-Sidney," and Smith has
enrolled his boys over sixteen into a company, with David
Witherspoon as lieutenant and Samuel Woodson Venable,
grandfather of the Chairman of your Faculty, as ensign;
and in 1777, the Governor calling for "Co. 1" of the
Prince Edward militia, we find the Rector-Captain advis-
ing the lads to exchange their number for "No. 1" with
the militia, and so presently they go marching gaily away
to Williamsburg, in their "hunting-shirts dyed purple,"
to meet a threatened invasion of the British.*

How vividly does all this recall to us, who were students here in '61, the stirring days when we too, emulous
of.the glories of our sires, marched away, one company
in Garibaldi shirts of red and one in soberer blue,† to give

---

*Foote, p. 400.

†In 1860-'61, two student-companies were enrolled at the University of
Virginia—"the Garibaldi Guard" (red shirts), Capt. Jas. T. Tosh, and
"the Southern Guard" (blue shirts), Capt. Edward S. Hutter, Jr. These
companies went to "the front" the night Virginia seceded. After the seizure
of Harper's Ferry, they returned to the University and disbanded, the
members *at once* enlisting in various commands. Five hundred out of the
six hundred students in the University enlisted *before June 1st*, 1861.

proof that we were true to our blood, and that the old spirit of '76 still pulsed bravely in the veins of those who had been jealously nurtured in the proud traditions bequeathed them by their fathers.

Yet something was done by dint of strenuous endeavor.

William and Mary carried on in a fashion its educational work until the seige of Yorktown, when it was temporarily closed to be used as a hospital for the sick and wounded, a purpose which it again served in 1861, and the academies of "Liberty Hall" and "Hampden-Sidney" flourished to some extent under the persistent efforts of Graham and John Blair Smith.

But the *Parsons' Schools* were well nigh swept away. The clergy of the Establishment were in the main loyal to the crown, only twenty-eight of the ninety-one* who held cures at the beginning of the struggle, remaining steadfast to their posts. Some, doubtless, resigned their charges, because they could no longer collect the stipend allowed them by law, and were thus forced to seek a livelihood elsewhere. But the majority were staunch Tories, and, making their way into the British lines, fared homewards.

In the excited state of the public mind, even those who remained faithful to the principles of the Revolution, were, in many instances, looked upon with suspicion, and shared most unjustly, as subsequent events proved, somewhat of the odium, which popular indignation directed against their class.†

Nearly all of them in time rose to be officers (two attaining the rank of Brigadier General). Many distinguished themselves conspicuously on the field and an appalling proportion were slain in battle.

¹*.*Meade*, I, 17.

†Yet, as Meade says, "there was a large share of noble patriotism in the clergy of Virginia. Mr. Jefferson declares this most emphatically." Meade, I, p. 266 sq. *Jeffersons Works*, I, pp. 5 and 6. One of the clergy, Rev. Arch'd McRoberts, Rector of St. Patrick's Parish, Prince Edward, in 1776 left the Establishment and embraced Presbyterianism. A curious case. See *Life of Rev. Devereux Jarratt*. *Meade*, I, p. 449.

Still here and there, is a gleam of light.

The Rev. Walker Maury, son of the James Maury, of whom I have spoken, was conducting a large and admirable classical school in Orange county, and having been induced to remove it to Williamsburg in 1782, as a sort of appendage to William and Mary College, where there was then no professor of "the Humanities," it speedily attained a great reputation for elegance and thoroughness of scholarship, not only in Virginia, but throughout all the Southern colonies. More than one hundred pupils were in attendance from Maryland to Georgia inclusive. There were four Assistant Masters, or ushers, as they were called, and the school appears to have been managed with great zeal and good judgment. The boys acted the plays of Plautus and Terence in the original, and were well drilled in Greek and in the easy Mathematics.* It was to this school, both while in Orange and afterwards in Williamsburg, that John Randolph of Roanoke, was sent, together with his older brothers, Richard and Theodorick.

Here pacing slowly around the statue of Lord Botetourt, then in the Old Capitol, he conned his "Westminster Greek Grammar" with such diligence as to be able to repeat it *verbatim* from cover to cover.

'Tis asserted that when the Latin comedies were acted, young Randolph was always chosen to play the female parts, for the alleged reason that "there was a spice of the devil in his temper." This is, of course, one of those gratuitous flings, which every masculine mind, in proper training, must at once reject. The probable reason for the choice lay in the fact that John Randolph with his liquid dark eyes, fringed with sweeping lashes, and his delicately chiselled features, was reckoned at the time the most beautiful boy in the school.

But dark as were the days for education during the

---

*Garland's *Life of John Randolph of Roanoke*, pp. 20, 21.

struggle for independence, still darker were the years suc-
ceeding the peace.

In 1782, Liberty Hall Academy was incorporated with
the right to give degrees, the first act of incorporation
granted by the Assembly after the virtual ending of the
Revolution ;* and, in the next year, Hampden Sidney obtained a charter as a college with the customary powers
and privileges. But both were in a depressed condition,
as was also William and Mary,† which suffered greatly

---

*Foote, p. 456. Touching the cost of tuition, about the time of the Rev-
olution, at these high schools (for they were nothing more), Foote says of
Liberty Hall : " During the first sixteen years of the Academy, tuition had
been forty shillings the session ; after the new buildings were prepared in
1794, the tuition was fifty shillings the session. From the tuition money
the salaries of all the teachers were to be paid. Some years he (Graham)
received nothing from the Academy," p. 476.

At Hampden Sidney, board, tuition, &c., for the year was £100 Virginia
money. See Foote, p. 401.

The poverty of the teachers of "ordinary" schools was proverbial.
Devereux Jarratt "hearing of a place in Albemarle—now Fluvanna—at a
Mr. Moon's, set out—his all, excepting only one shirt, being on his back,
and that which was in his hand was lost soon after." Meade, 1, p. 470.
Life of Rev. Devereux Jarrett. Drury Lacy (born 1758), of Chesterfield,
who went for a short time to a noted boarding-school in Powhatan, kept
by Rev. Mr. McRea, an Episcopal clergyman, was employed by his poor
neighbors to teach a school, when he was but sixteen. " I have heard him
remark," says his son, " that so very limited were his means, that he was
under the necessity of walking barefoot to and from the school-house.
The covering for his head a rough straw-hat." (Quoted by Foote, p. 491.)
Lacy was, however, a determined student, became tutor in Hampden-Sidney College and afterwards Vice-President (exercising all the functions of
President) of that institution. Foote, p. 497. The condition of teachers
of such schools was no better in New England. See McMaster's Hist. of
the People of the United States, vol. i, p. 21 sqq.

†See Foote, 403. La Rochefoucault, as late as 1796, says : " There is no
State so entirely destitute of all means of public education as Virginia,
and it may be fairly said that the only college she possesses is the most
imperfect in point of instruction and the worst managed of any in the
Union." Travels through the United States of North America, etc., by the
Duke de la Rochefoucault Liancourt (London, 1799), vol. iii, p. 227.
Touching the expences of students at William and Mary, he says that the
total "expence to their parents amounts to about a hundred and sixty or a
hundred and seventy dollars a year." III, p. 49.

from being generally reputed a centre of deism and the hot-bed of all those wild French socialistic ideas,[*] which within ten years were to flame out in mad fury in the country which gave them birth, send Louis Capet to the guillotine, and plunge the fair land of our allies into all the sanguinary horrors of "the Terror."

Undoubtedly, the financial distress just after the close of the war, and, indeed, for years after, had much to do with the general apathy touching education.

Many gentlemen, who had left good estates in flourishing condition when they rode away to join the army, found themselves well-nigh ruined on their return, through the long neglect of their business, the loss of their negroes, who had been run off by the British, and the wasteful mismanagement of overseers. The men, who had been in a way, the patrons of learning, were harassed by debt and were daily growing more impoverished owing to the low price of tobacco.[†]   A fever of speculation had seized upon

---

[*]*Meade*, I, p. 29 ; II, p. 292 and elsewhere.   The college was also in bad repute on the score of alleged dissipation.   That it long enjoyed this reputation, may be seen from the following passage in a curious little book, which has recently come into my hands.   The author is said in the " Translator's Preface " to be " a young Frenchman of ancient family," who came to Virginia in the early years of the present century :

" Harry Whiffler, I believe, was born somewhere in the county of King and Queen.   His father was a rich planter in that quarter, who, somehow or other, took a notion in his head, that it would be a very clever thing to bring his son up to the trade and mystery of a gentleman.   He was accordingly sent, in due time, to the college of William and Mary, where he soon went through the whole circle of *vices* taught in that polite seminary.   It is true he didn't make quite so great a progress in the sciences.   He passed, however, for a lad of great genius, principally upon the ground of his laziness.   For it was observed, that he played cards all night and lay abed all day, and, therefore, according to the logic of the place, it was justly inferred that he must have brilliant talents, if he could only be prevailed upon to show 'em."   *Letters from Virginia.* Transl. from the French (Balto., 1816), p. 53.   The author describes his visit to the college in " letter xv" (p. 124 *sqq.*), ascribing its deplorable condition of decay to the prevalence of rampant infidelity and unrestrained dissipation.

[†]*McMaster's Hist. People of U. S.*, vol. i, p. 273.

them, who, on the failure of the wild ventures upon which *many* they had embarked, were plunged into hopeless bankruptcy.

Bad as had been the morals of the old " Parsons," their loss, from an educational point of view, was now grievously felt.

Their places were taken in a measure by Scotch and Irish dominies, graduates of Glasgow and Aberdeen, and of Trinity College, Dublin, who came over in considerable numbers on the conclusion of the peace.

Most of them were sound scholars and established schools of good repute in Norfolk, Richmond, and other towns. They seemed to have been distinguished for three things—an accurate knowledge of Latin prosody, a fervent belief in the efficacy of the rod, and a love of drink.

Well do I remember, as a boy, hearing from an old gentleman* on the lower James an account of his school life " in the nineties " under the Scotch tutor, whom his father employed to teach his own children and those of the neighboring planters—a notable Greek and Latin scholar and a zealous disciple of the "baculine" method. There was a morning and afternoon session, the school being dismissed for dinner from one until three. According to the universal custom in those hospitable old days, a great bowl of rum-punch was every day at noon placed upon the side-board in the dining-room, and all who chose, young and old, might help themselves. During the morning session, the dominie was alert and would pounce upon the luckless victim, who stammered over his Euclid or made a false quantity, with the awful brow of Jove himself. Then came the recess, when the chief delight of the boys was to watch the frequent surreptitious visits of the dominie to the dining-room "to see whether dinner was ready."

At dinner again, there was crusty port and Madeira,

*Dr. John Minge, formerly of Weyanoke on James River.

5

which had "doubled the Cape," on the excellences of which the discriminating Scot was wont to enlarge until the tears stood in his eyes.

At three, began the afternoon session.

At first, there was a studied precision of movement and great affectation of vigilance, but alas, like honest Bardolph, "his zeal burnt only in his nose"—thicker and thicker grew the native burr, gradually the master's explanations became more and more incoherent, until, finally, his head fell gently on his breast, and, like the grooms in Macbeth, he "mocked his charge with snores."

Day after day this went on, yet the boys, I was told, learned fairly well, and, such were the lax notions of the time as to drinking, that the only notice of it was a laugh at the dominie for not having a stronger head.

Mr. Jefferson,* it is true, as far back as 1779, in conjunction with his co-revisors of our laws — Pendleton and Wythe — drew up and submitted to the General Assembly a plan for a general system of education, providing for the establishment of three classes of seminaries :

1. *Elementary Schools*, to be maintained at the public charge and *free to all*.

2. *General Schools*, corresponding to academies and colleges, for the education of such as had time, means and inclination for further culture, to be assisted to some extent from the public treasury, but to be supported chiefly by the fees of the pupils.

---

*The statements in the text touching Mr. Jefferson's efforts to promote education in Virginia are based on Tucker's and Randall's lives of Jefferson, the "*Correspondence of Jefferson and Cabell*" and "*A Sketch of the University of Virginia*" (Richmond : 1885), ascribed to Professor Jno. B. Minor, LL. D., of the University. At the time the address was written, Dr. Herbert Adams's admirable monograph, "*Thomas Jefferson and the University of Virginia*," (Washington : 1888) had not yet appeared. Dr. Adams' work must rank as the definitive history of our University and entitles him to the lasting gratitude of every Virginian.

3. *An University*, in which should be taught in the highest degree every branch of knowledge.

The plan thus submitted was not even considered by the Assemby until 1796, when, owing to what the first Governor John Tyler calls "the shameful parsimony of the legislature,"[*] only that portion of the bill relating to Elementary Schools was adopted, and that with such amendments as made it almost barren of results.

But from 1784 to 1816, we find on our statute books no less than seventeen acts authorizing the raising of money by lotteries for the establishment or maintenance of academies in various parts of the State.[†]

Some of these appear to have enjoyed a considerable popularity for a time, and a few of them prolonged a precarious existence into "the thirties," but none were of conspicuous merit. These, were doubtless, "the paltry academies," over whose inefficiency Mr. Jefferson utters his moan.

From 1801 to 1809, Jefferson was busied with national affairs as President of the United States, but on his retirement into private life in the latter year, though we find him writing to his friend, John Tyler, that his mind is "dissolved in tranquillity,"[‡] his correspondence proves that he had by no means relinquished his scheme for education, formulated thirty years before, which ever lay closest to his heart in his lusty old age. Could he but see an efficient system of general education firmly established, he was ready, he declared, to say with old Simeon, "*Nunc demittas, Domine.*"[||]

Through the enlightened and persistent efforts of Tyler,

---

[*]*Letters and Times of the Tylers*, by Lyon G. Tyler (Richmond : 1884), vol. i, p. 237.

[†]See *Jefferson's Correspondence*, iv, p. 430 sqq.

[‡]*Letters and Times of the Tylers*, i, p. 248.

[||]*Jeff. Corresp.*, iv, p. 341.

then Governor of the State, who, as a member of the legislature, had enthusiastically supported the plan submitted in '79, a bill drawn by James Barbour,* the Speaker of the House, was reported in January 1810 for the establishment of the "Literary Fund," and enacted into a law on February 2nd of the same year.

This was by far the most important and far-reaching of all the acts of the legislature touching education up to that time. Five years later, in February 1815, a resolution, " undoubtedly inspired by Jefferson,"† directed "the President and Directors of the Literary Fund" to elaborate a system of public instruction, and in December of the next year they made a report, recommending a scheme essentially the same in many respects as that proposed in 1779. A bill, embodying the recommendation, was passed by the House, but defeated by the Senate on the ground that the sense of the people should be taken on a matter involving so great an expenditure of the public money.‡

Undeterred by this second failure, Mr. Jefferson again prepared a third bill, which he trusted would reconcile the conflicting views of all parties. His scheme was not wholly adopted, yet far more was gained than in 1796, for the act of 1818, while appropriating the greater portion of the income from the "Literary Fund" to the establishment of Elementary Schools for the poor, gave $15,000 a year to endow and support a University to be styled "THE UNIVERSITY OF VIRGINIA."

Before this, Mr. Jefferson and some of his neighbors had undertaken to revive the declining "Albemarle Academy" by liberal private subscriptions, and with such success, that, on Jefferson's suggestion, the original plan was enlarged, and the academy incorporated as "Central College" in

---

*Letters and Times of the Tylers, i, p. 242.

†Sketch of Univ. of Va., p. 6.

‡Tucker's Life of Jefferson, ii, p. 399.

February 1816. This may be regarded as in some sort the germ of our present University.

On January 25th, 1819, a date never to be forgotten, the University of Virginia was established by act of Assembly, and, from that time until his death in 1826, engrossed to the exclusion of all else the time and thoughts of the foremost man of his age.

Thus, finally was laid the foundation of real university education, not only in Virginia, but in America.*

The condition of education in Virginia during the first quarter of the present century may be clearly traced in the correspondence of Jefferson with Joseph Cabell and with other friends, which draws such a picture of the inefficiency of our schools and colleges, as makes one doubt whether there was not sounder teaching in the colony from 1700—1725 than in the commonwealth from 1800 to 1825.

During all this period great numbers of our lads were sent North to be educated in the schools of New England, notably at the celebrated Phillips Academy at Exeter (N. H.), and Jefferson bewails in one of his letters that half of the students at Princeton were Virginians.†

As late as 1820, we find him writing to Cabell: "The mass of education in Virginia before the Revolution placed her with the foremost of her sister colonies. What is her education now? Where is it? The little we have, we import like beggars from other States; or import their beggars to bestow on us their miserable crumbs."‡

The beggars, whom we imported to bestow on us their miserable crumbs, were, of course, "the Yankee schoolmasters," who, from 1810 to 1830, came down in swarms from New England to Virginia and could be found in every town and well nigh in every county of the State.

---

*Adams, *The College of William and Mary*, p. 12.

†*Jeff. Corresp.* iv, p. 340.

‡*Ib.* iv, p. 334.

As I have spoken bluntly of the old Parsons, it is due the truth of our educational history that I should speak with like freedom of these later apostles of learning. Some of them were men of high character and fair attainments, and founded families of great respectability in this state. But it is simple truth to declare that the great body of them were not men to inspire respect for their calling either by their learning or their bearing.

"Why he calls us '*fellows*,'" was the astonished and delighted exclamation of a Rugby lad soon after Arnold's first coming to that school as head-master, and, in this hearty use of the familiar name employed among themselves, we recognize the great school-master's instinctive knowledge of how simply the love and confidence of boys may be won and held.

But there was nothing of this sort among the precise and formal pedagogues, who presided over our Virginia schools. No boy was called by the familiar home-name of " Jim ' or "Tom," but "James" and "Thomas" with a precision of nasal intonation, that would suggest to the least imaginative the ghostly glitter of "skeleton spectacles," long-fingered black-gloves, and a Pecksniffian snuffle. Their pronunciation of Latin was, like Byron's prosody at Harrow, "such as pleased God," and they were as ignorant of Greek accents or the nicer points of Greek syntax as they were of the Talmud.

Touching the management of boys, they brought with them all the detestable traditions of the colleges, where they had been trained.

They prided themselves on their slyness in espionage, and put a premium on lying by attempting to compel a boy when "caught in a scrape" to "peach" on his comrades.

They delivered themselves of long homilies on the sinfulness of fighting and tried to persuade healthy and high-spirited lads that the distinctive mark of perfect gentleman-hood, was, when smitten one cheek, to meekly turn the other. The boys, of course, listened demurely in public to these dreary moral platitudes and guffawed over them in private ; and as soon as the master's back was turned, if Master Jack or Tom had any little account to be settled, they slipped off their jackets and "had it out," as I trust all true Virginia lads of grit will ever do.

The boys despised rather than hated them. These were the days of "barring out" and wonderful "cold-water traps" for deluging the teacher in his sudden nightly raids into dormitories, and all the other ingenious devices that our fathers have gleefully described to us, whereby they made wretched the hapless New England pedagogue, who commonly revenged himself for the contemptuous insubor-dination of the older boys by unmercifully thrashing the smaller ones.

In December 1825, Jefferson, writing to Wm. B. Giles, afterwards Governor of the state, says : "I learn with great satisfaction that your school is thriving well and that you have at its head a truly classical scholar. *He is one of the three or four whom I can hear of in the State.* We were obliged last year to receive shameful Latinists into the classical school of the University ; such as we will cer-tainly refuse as soon as we can get from better schools a sufficiency of those properly instructed to form a class. We must get rid of this Connecticut Latin, of this barba-rous confusion of long and short syllables, which renders doubtful whether we are listening to a reader of Cherokee, Shawnee, Iroquois, or what."* The "better schools," of which this broad statesman and accomplished scholar speaks, were to come in good time.

*/b., iv, p. 423. Col. Frank Ruffin informs me that that the "truly classi-cal scholar" was Mr. Bartholomew Egan, an Englishman and graduate of an English University.

Owing to lack of money, six years had been consumed in the erection of the necessary buildings here, but on March 5th, 1825, the University of Virginia, with a faculty small, indeed, but the ablest in America, threw open its doors for students.

Thither, in 1832, came FREDERICK WILLIAM COLEMAN, third son of Thomas Burbidge* Coleman and Elizabeth Lindsey Coghill, of the County of Caroline.

Such preparation as he had for college, he owed partly to private study, partly to his father, who at the time was conducting a school of good local repute on his estate, known as "Concord." He was sprung, indeed, from a family of teachers. His grand-father, Daniel Coleman, who had been an officer in the Revolution, taught a school for many years after the peace at Concord, was succeeded by Frederick's father, Thomas, who, in turn, was succeeded by his sons, Atwell and James. Frederick Coleman himself had also taught in his father's school before coming to the University. The methods of instruction were those of the ordinary Virginia "country school," and Frederick Coleman, in after years, would amuse his pupils with a hundred droll stories illustrative of his crass ignorance when he entered college.†

Before coming of age, he had settled upon teaching as his profession, and it was better to qualify himself for his chosen calling, that he came to the University, which, owing to the care and discretion exercised by Jefferson in the selection of its first faculty, had achieved at a single bound, as it were, a great reputation, and made its claim assured to the first place in the higher education of Virginia.

He was just twenty-one‡ when he matriculated, and I

* The name is commonly spelled "Burbage," but Mrs. Alice Coleman DeJarnette writes me that it is properly Burbidge.
†MS. letter of Prof. Edward S. Joynes of Univ. of South Carolina.
‡Born Aug. 3rd., 1811.

am told by one who was his closest college friend, that he was at that time an almost perfect type of Herculean young manhood—six feet, two inches in height, deep of chest and long of limb, "a fellow of infinite jest," the soul of every company with his "quaint flashes of merriment," yet withal possessed of a strong passion for scholarship. Nothing could more fully illustrate the vigor of his acquisitive powers than the surprising facility with which he rid himself of the old educational modes practiced at his father's school, and mastered the more scientific methods of his new and better-trained instructors.

Within a brief time he was in all his classes a man of mark, and, after three years of unbroken success, was graduated Master of Arts.

The period of his residence here as an undergraduate was one of high political excitement throughout the country, and, eager student as he was, Frederick Coleman, with native Virginian aptitude for politics, did not escape the contagion.

His father, who represented his county for twenty consecutive years in the Virginia Assembly, was a "Jeffersonian Democrat" of the straitest sect, and naturally the son had been bred in the faith of "strict construction." Within two months of his matriculation, South Carolina had passed the ordinance of Nullification, and not even in 1860 was there fiercer contention in Congress, or bitterer animosity in humbler debate than everywhere prevailed in '32 and '33.

"Nullification," "the Force Bill," "Compromise Tariff," "the Removal of the Deposits"—such were the questions, which threatened to rend asunder the nation, and men, North and South, hung with bated breath on the utterances of the mighty gladiatorial trio, who had stepped into the arena, and who in the council chamber of the nation were debating with keenest logic and matchless eloquence the issues at stake.

The head of the Law School here at the time was John A. G. Davis, a man of high spirit and notable ability, who taught the law as a code of principles rather than a line of precedents. Chief in importance o (the departments of his chair was Constitutional Law. The text-books were the Federalist and what were then known as "the immortal Resolutions of '98 and '99" and the debates thereon.* As in the stirring autumn of 1860 students "cut" their lectures in the Academic Department to throng the lecture-room of Jas. P. Holçombe, so, in those exciting days of '33, was Davis's lecture-room crowded with eager youths, who came to hear him discuss the question which Calhoun and Webster were debating on a larger field— whether the Constitution was a simple compact or a fundamental law; and, among all his enthusiastic audience, there was no keener listener than Frederick Coleman, who applauded in uproarious fashion, as the Professor, arguing on historical premises, taught absolute denial of the supremacy of the United States Courts in fixing by construction the rights of a state.†

At that time he became what he remained to his dying day, an enthusiastic politician, and if his boys did not imbibe strict "States Rights doctrine," it was not for lack of hearing it vigorously preached.

In 1835, on his graduation, he joined his brother, Atwell, in the conduct of the school in Caroline, and called it "Concord Academy," the name by which it afterwards became so famous throughout the whole Southern country.

Within a year or two, his brother removed to Alabama, and Frederick Coleman became sole proprietor.

He at once swept away every vestige of the old order

*Letter of Col. Frank G. Ruffin.
†*Ib.*

of things, discarding, as I have said, with a contempt characteristic of the imperious nature of the man, all the traditional methods of discipline.

That he erred in going as far as he did in this direction, none can now deny, but there was everything in the detestable methods of the old system to provoke a man of his temperament to such sweeping iconoclasm.

He had had recent experience at the University of the evils resulting from a multiplication of rules and regulations,* and this experience, added to his inbred impatience

---

*Mr. Jefferson's policy as regards discipline in the University contemplated the largest liberty to the students, but the latter through a mistaken view of what was expected of them under his system of self-goverment did not respond to the appeals made " to " their reason, their hopes, and their generous feelings. Lawlessness and riot were for a time rife in the institution and became so intolerable that the professors suspended their lectures and tendered their resignations to the Board of Visitors. The Board met, abandoned the plan of self-government, and ordered a course of rigid discipline to be pursued. As was, perhaps, natural under the circumstances, the Faculty, in the exercise of their new powers, and smarting under the provocation they had received, erred in going to the opposite extreme of punishing light offenses with unnecessary severity. Things went on thus for several years, the gulf growing wider and wider between the students and professors, until matters finally culminated in the once celebrated, but now forgotten " Rebellion of '34." (See letter of Mr. William Wertenbaker, for nearly half a century Librarian of the University, published in Ingram's *Edgar Allan Poe*, vol. i, pp. 44, 45.) I cannot do better than give in Col. Ruffin's own words an account of this " Rebellion of '34 " as stated to me in his letter of April 11th, 1888 : " In that year Professor Bonnycastle, then chairman of the Faculty, upon the occasion of some slight and now forgotten irregularity, got the Faculty to pass an order that the students, at the sounding of the 9 P. M. bell, should retire to their rooms, there to remain until six o'clock next morning. Immediately upon the promulgation of this order, the students met and a large majority (including those who boarded out of the college limits, all of whom were required to be twenty years of age) resolved and sent a copy of their resolution to the Faculty, that they would disobey the order. Upon this, the Faculty notified them that, if they did not repeal their resolution and apologize for their conduct, they would be expelled. The students refused positively to yield. At this stage, the Chaplain, at the instance of the Faculty, interposed and the affair was arranged by the Faculty's withdrawing their demand. I never saw proceedings conducted in a more orderly way." Col. Ruffin's letter gives a most interesting sketch of student-life at the University from 1832 to 1838.

of all conventionality and restraint, determined him on
trying the bold experiment of giving his pupils such a
share of personal liberty as no school-boys had ever before
enjoyed. Above all, he was resolved that the unwritten
law of personal honor, and not the fear of punishment,
should be the controlling power of the school.

A favorite pupil of his, Master of Arts of this University, now a distinguished professor in another, thus describes to me his first impressions of " Concord :"*

" ' Concord Academy ' was a massive brick building,
surrounded by a few log-cabins, situated absolutely in the
' old fields '—no inclosures—no flowery walks—no attraction for the eye, such as I had been accustomed to in the
academies I had attended at the North. Within, all was
rude and rough—the barest necessities of decent furni-
ture—the table abundant, but coarsely served—the rooms
devoid of all luxury or grace—no trace of feminine art,
nor sound of woman's voice to relieve the first attacks of
home-sickness—everything rough, severe, masculine.

" I looked and inquired after the ' Rules and Regulations '
of the School. I found there were none ! To my horror
I felt deserted even by the eye of discipline. It seemed
to me the reign of lawlessness with utter desolation and
loneliness. But soon I found that there reigned at ' Concord ' the one higher law : *Be a man !*—that what I thought
solitude and helplessness, was the lesson of individuality :
Be yourself. As for discipline there was none in the usual
sense of the term. *Be a man—Be a gentleman*—nothing
more. Far too little, indeed nothing at all of those rules,
those proprieties, those methods that belong to the well-
regulated school.

" *Obedience* and *truthfulness* were the only virtues recog-

*Prof. Edward S. Joynes, M. A., LL. D., of the University of South
Carolina, whose charming sketch of his school-boy life at Concord and of
"Old Fred" (contained in a long letter to me March 25th, 1888) is well
worthy of publication.

nized or inculcated at Concord: *obedience absolute* to
Frederick Coleman — his will was law, was gospel, was
'Concord.' There was not a boy, even of those that loved
him most, who did not fear him absolutely. And *truthfulness with courage.* All else was forgiven but lying and
cowardice. These were *not forgiven*, for they were im-
possible at Concord."

Not less extraordinary was the absence of all rules in
regard to the preparation of tasks and hours of recitation.
The boys studied when and where they chose, and the
length of time given to a class varied from thirty minutes
to three hours, according to the judgment of the instructor.

Boys were knocked up at all hours of the night, sometimes long after midnight, and summoned to the recitation-
room by " Old Ben," the faithful negro janitor, who equally
feared and worshipped his master. A sharp rap at the
door, and the familiar cry, " Sophocles, with your candles,
young gentlemen," would send the youngsters tumbling
out of bed in the long winter nights, just as they had
begun to dream of home or of certain bright eyes that had
bewitched them in the " long vacation." " Many and many
a time," says Dr. Joynes, " each fellow with his tallow dip,
have we read till long past midnight and never a sleepy
eye, while ' Old Fred ' expounded to us Antigone or Ajax."
" Old Ben " is a character, which I should love to dwell
on, did time allow. His pronunciation of the names of
Latin and Greek authors was, I am told, open to criticism,
but Frederick Coleman's old boys have a hundred stories
illustrative of his fidelity to his master and his canine instinct in tracking the boys to their haunts, whenever they
were wanted.

Professor Gray Carroll, who took a brilliant Master's
degree here in '55, tells me that on one occasion, Mr.
Coleman, in giving out the lesson, inadvertently announced
the wrong day for the next recitation. The class deter-

mined to take advantage of his absentmindedness and go
fishing. No band of Italian conspirators ever exercised
more ingenuity in hoodwinking the. Papal police, than did
these alert youngsters in concealing their preparations
from "Old Ben." Silently and swiftly they sped away
one by one to the trysting place two miles distant, and
were just casting their lines, with many a chuckle over
their prospective holiday, when their blood was frozen by
the terribly familiar cry : "'Ripides,* young gen'l'men,
right away, Mars' Fred is waitin'." Fate in the person of
"Old Ben" was too much for them, and the little proces-
sion sadly wended its way back to the class-room.

The law of *place* was as uncertain as that of *time*, and, in
the long summer days, "Old Fred," in such scanty attire
as would have shocked the sensibilities of Mr. Anthony
Comstock, surrounded by his eager pupils clad in like slender raiment, would lie on the soft sward under the great
trees and "hold high converse with the mighty dead."

But whatever the hour or the place, all who knew him,
hold him the greatest teacher of his time.

Governor John L. Marye, who entered Concord in 1838,
writes to me : "My schooling up to that time had been
under the tuition of the old-fashioned teachers, chiefly imported from the North. Going from a *town* and having
been for five years under the instruction (!) of what was
dubbed 'The Classical and Mathematical Academy' of
Fredericksburg, I entered Concord with some complacent
idea as to my comparative scholarship with that of the
average boy. You will not doubt that my *first* experiences
as a pupil under Mr. Coleman were a startling and hum-
bling revelation to my young and callow mind. My recol-
lection is that he succeeded on the *very first day* of my
appearing in class before him in convincing me that much
which I valued as my *acquirements* had to be summarily *un-*

*This was Ben's pronunciation of the name of a certain Greek dramatist.

learned. Then followed day by day that exhibition by him of the elevated, enlightened and philosophical method of instruction, which marked his teaching and made his school the pioneer in the grand line of Academies, which followed in Virginia."

Professor Edward Joynes, whom I have already quoted, says :

" Frederick Coleman's teaching! What was it? Wherein its magic power? Why is it still famous after forty years, so that like Nestor μετὰ τριτάτοισιν ἀνάσσει. Ah! I cannot tell you. I cannot analyze or describe it. I only know that I have seen no such teaching since, and I have sat at the feet of Harrison and Courtenay and McGuffey at home, and of Haupt and Boeckh and Bopp abroad. It was just the immeasurable force of supreme intellect and will, that entered into you and *possessed* you, until it seemed that every fibre of your brain obeyed his impulse. Like the ' Ancient Mariner,' he ' held you with his glittering eye ' and like him ' he had his will ' with you. If I should try to define its *spirit*, it would be by the word *self-forget-fulness*—the complete absorption of Coleman himself, and so, by his supreme will-power, of his whole class, in the subject in hand, so that every power of attention, intelligence, sympathy, was controlled by him to the work of the hour. If then I should try in a word to define its *method*, it would be concentration. *Non multa, sed multum.* He held that the first ' Book ' of Livy contained all Latinity, and that 'all the glory that was Greece' was to be found in the *Hecuba* of Euripides. These were his *pièces de résistance*, and he taught them as they were never taught before or since. From these as centres or starting points, his teaching of Latin and Greek proceeded. A copy of the *Hecuba*, for instance, as taught by Coleman would be a literary curiosity. Every line, phrase, idiom was made a centre of citation ranging far and wide over the plays (we used only the complete texts without "notes" at Concord). " *Where does this occur elsewhere ?*" " *Where, otherwise ?*" " *What is the difference ?*" " *What is the point thus differentiated or illustrated ?*" "*Why ?*" — until the margin could hardly hold his references.

" But, indeed, Frederick Coleman's teaching cannot be analyzed except by saying that it was Frederick Coleman himself. He was a man of massive power of *body*, *mind*, *will*. Through this power he dominated his boys — impressed himself upon them—wrought himself into them— controlled them by his mighty will-power — roused them by his mighty sympathy.

" As a teacher, he was the greatest of his age — there has been no other like him."

As will be noted above, he used in Latin and Greek only the complete texts of the Tauchnitz editions, without notes, and was wont to inveigh with sarcastic vigor against what John Randolph called "the Yankee editions" of the classics — which is scarcely to be wondered at, when we remember that the best of them then were those edited by Dr. Anthon, whose books a wicked *Saturday Reviewer* once described as "a not first-rate store-house of second-hand German learning."

Like Arnold's, his temper, when aroused, was furious, and the stoutest-hearted lad quailed before it. Against anything that savored of baseness or meanness, his indignation rose quickly and mounted swiftly to intense passion. Two things, as we have been told, he would never forgive—lying and cowardice. He accepted a lad's word implicitly, and if he tampered with truth, he must go. Fighting he allowed, of course. He was always ready to mediate, and, if that failed, he was equally ready to see that the fight was a fair one. Bullying he put down with a stern hand. If, after the fight, anything remained unforgiven, he would adjudicate, and the boys must shake hands.*

The whole nature of the man was instinct with honesty and truth, and his high personal courage was proverbial. One of the traditions gloried in by Concord boys, who worshipped him as a mightier hero than Telamonian Ajax or any of their favorite "Three Musketeers," was of the day, famous in the annals of Caroline, when Frederick Coleman and his younger brother vanquished single-handed six strapping rustic bullies, who had long been the terror of the court-green.

Thus, without any law or method, the foundations were laid of that noble *esprit* in morals and thoroughness in scholarship, which made "Concord" the most famous of Virginia schools. The secret of his success lay in the strong boyish element in his nature, which is a marked characteristic of so many men of high ability.

"His relations with his boys out of school," says one of old pupils,† "was not only one of absolute equality, but of *bonhomie*—of intimacy and familiarity—yet such as none could ever dare abuse."

"His whole life," says another,‡ "was spent with his boys, and his interest in their work and amusements and *in them personally* was felt by all to be genuine and unaffected. He seemed to know, almost intuitively, the character and mental peculiarities of every boy, and found time to adapt his admonition or instruction to each one individually, as if his whole business was to make the most that was possible of that particular boy."

"His mind was richly stored with knowledge of many things and his thought was always vigorous and original. His conversation was a never ending pleasure to his boys.

---

*Professor Joynes's letter.

†Professor Joynes.

‡Professor Gray Carroll. Dr. J. R. Baylor writes me to the same effect.

Sometimes he would join a knot of them sitting in the shade on a summer evening and enter with them into the discussion of any subject that happened to engage their attention at the moment. Presently the discussion would become a monologue. Parties engaged at play in different parts of the grounds would drop their bats or their marbles and silently gather around. Before long, it would become known from room to room that 'Old Fred is talking' and the whole school would be collected about him, listening with such charmed intentness to his words, that even the sound of the supper bell was regarded as an unwelcome interruption. His talk on these occasions was solid and instructive, and he never made the mistake of talking below the intelligence of his hearers. He did not adapt his conversation to them ; he raised their minds to the level of his own thoughts."

" Sometimes, it would be his humor to encourage boys to talk, and, while taking his full share in the fun and repartee, I do not doubt that he was gathering valuable lessons about the character and understanding of the boys engaged, and the state of the public sentiment in the school. These helps to success he had and many more, but above and beyond them all, was his great unselfish heart — a heart large enough and tender enough to take in the joys and sorrows of all about him. We all felt this, and I suppose no other teacher was ever so fully admitted into the confidence of his boys."

Unquestionably, there was much in the school open to grave criticism : the large liberty allowed the boys, amounted almost to license—there was a general lack of punctuality and method in the conduct of the school, until Lewis Coleman came as Assistant Master in 1846—the classing of boys was largely governed by chance, instead of being based upon careful preliminary examination*—

*Professor Gray Carroll and Dr. J. R. Baylor.

there was no environment of those refining influences, which have no mean share in determining character.

Mr. Coleman was himself naturally impatient of all conventionality and restraint, and his *unconscious* disregard of the minor *convenances* of life was *consciously* cultivated by ardent disciples, who worshipped him and made him their model.

As Oxford men, fifty years ago, were wont to declare of Arnold's pupils in the University that they affected, in imitation of their master, "earnestness" (with a big E) in the most trivial matters, and were "a lot" of solemn young prigs, so it was said here at this University that the boys, who came up from "Concord" aped Frederick Coleman and cultivated a roughness of manner and carelessness of attire but little engaging.

But fortunate was it for Virginia that just when the public mind was ripe for revolt from the old systems of discipline and of teaching, a man of such sound scholarship and high personal character, with such intuition of boyish nature and faith in boyish love of truth, should have risen up in our midst to found a school, which should give the death-blow to the old sluggish and pernicious methods, and fix the standard of secondary education in the State.

There might be criticism of the roughness of their manners, but there was no question here, the court of final appeal, as to the superiority of "Concord boys" in the domain of scholarship, or of their scorn of all that savored of dishonor.

It was a grand old school, and, as a Virginia schoolmaster, I uncover and salute it.

The reputation of Frederick Coleman as a wonderful talker has come down to us, and many stories are still told of the originality and cleverness of his conversation. Like old Sam Johnson, he was imperious and dogmatic in his manner, impatient of dissent where his convictions were deep, rapid in articulation, warming up to vehemence in voice and gesture as his interest kindled, yet withal with such kindliness and honesty shining through the rugged lines of his face as made one forget the sting of occasional sarcasm and remember only the charm of the wonderful monologue. Great as was the divergence in character between the two men, one is constantly reminded of Colet in listening to the descriptions of Frederick Coleman as given by his old pupils — "his lively conversation, his frank simplicity, the purity and nobleness of his life, even the keen outbursts of his troublesome temper, endeared him " to all.*

The ladies in my audience may be interested to know that Frederick Coleman's admiration of the gentler sex was such as can be measured by no poor rhetoric of mine— such as can only be represented by algebraic formulæ, in which m and n are as conspicuous as in the Church Catechism. In every section of the state at various times, he "*met his fate*," and, though he never married, was in a chronic state of " sighing like a furnace."

In 1849, after fifteen years of unparallelled success, he suddenly determined to close the school. He urged many reasons for the step to his intimates, who remonstrated against his purpose. He had grown to be distressingly obese and began to worry about his health. Despite his open-handed liberality, where money was in question, he had amassed an easy competence—above all, he was anxious to push the fortunes of his favorite pupil and nephew, Lewis Coleman, who had determined to establish a school of like grade in Hanover.

He met all remonstrances with a glowing picture of the delights of a serene old age passed among his books, and the sweet converse of cultured friends.

But it is the old story.

*Green's Short History of the English People, p. 317.

Enforced idleness chafed the restless spirit. In the sluggish leisure of prosaic daily life, he recognized no trace of the charm of the "lettered ease" of his dreams. He entered political life, served a single term in the State Senate, tired of it, and declined re-election.

Too late he recognized the mistake of having surrendered his work in the fulness of his powers, and I am told by those who knew him well that he became moody and melancholy.

His life thenceforth was uneventful. The war came, but he could take no part in it, and we can well imagine how galling that was to a man of his high spirit and strong convictions as to the justice and right of our contention.

He survived the issue of the war but a few years, dying peacefully at Fredericksburg in 1868.

The year in which "Concord" closed its doors, saw the establishment of "Hanover Academy" in the county of that name by Lewis Minor Coleman.

I can glance but briefly at his life.

He was the eldest son of Thomas Burbidge Coleman, Jr., and of Mary Coleman his wife, and was born in the county of Hanover, February 3rd., 1827.

His father, a fine type of the Virginia country squire and long a representative of his county in the Assembly, died in the prime of life leaving three small children to be reared by the mother.

Fortunately, she was well qualified for the task.

According to the universal testimony of those who knew her, she was a noble type of the Virginia matron—vigorous in mind and character, highly educated and an enthusiastic lover of books—ready in her sympathies and of great tenderness of heart; yet a woman of notable firmness and energy, and possessed of that "soft invincibility" of purpose, which was such a marked characteristic of her noble son.

She gave up her whole life to her children and grounded Lewis thoroughly in English and in the rudiments of Latin.

Repeatedly in after years, he declared that whatever of good there was in his life or character, he owed to the careful training of this mother.

When fourteen he was sent for a year to a private school at Col. Fontaine's in Hanover, and the next year entered "Concord."

He was then a lad of ardent and generous nature, and of acquirement far beyond his years. Apart from the clannish affection which he felt for all who shared his blood, Frederick Coleman, who took but little interest in a stupid boy,* was fairly captivated by the cleverness of his brilliant young kinsman. With his quick intuition of the capacities of boys, he saw that this cleverness was no superficial precocity, but that the lad had in him the stuff of a real scholar. From that time down to the day of his death, Lewis Coleman was son rather than nephew to the master of Concord.

Within a few months. he went to the top of the school and staid there. Yet none of his fellows envied him his high rank in the school, for with his bright and lively temperament, his boyish ardor for all manly sports, his high courage and steadfast loyalty in friendship, he was a true "boy's boy," and was as mnch looked up to on the play-ground as in the class-room.

At seventeen he entered the University, graduated in four "schools"† his first year, and at the close of the second (in 1846) was graduated Master of Arts.

In the autumn following his graduation, he returned to Concord as Assistant Master. He was but nineteen and

---

*Letter of Dr. John Roy Baylor.

†The "schools" at the University in which he graduated the first year were Latin, Greek, (then one "school," under title of "Ancient Languages") French, Mathematics, and Moral Philosophy.

the position in most cases would have been a trying one.
Many of the boys in the school were as old as he, and
some of them had been his schoolfellows. Yet, even at that
early age, he displayed such a happy knack in winning the
respect and confidence of his pupils, that they soon became as enthusiastic in their loyalty to him as to the head-
master of the school.

Thus, when three years later he established the new
school, it was essentially but a more orderly development
of the old. "Concord" had simply been removed from
Caroline to Hanover.

As an old "Concord" boy, he had seen the splendid
results of Frederick Coleman's noble experiment in trust-
ing the moral government of the school to the sentiment
of personal honor, and he was resolved to make what was
then first known as "the honor system" the chief corner-
stone of the new foundation. Happily more than half the
pupils enrolled the first session at "Hanover" were old
"Concord" boys, and thus at the outset was fixed without
any trouble on his part the tone of public sentiment in the
school.

But despite his loyalty and reverence for his old master
and kinsman, he had seen the faults in the conduct of the
old school, and wisely determined to make many modifications of the careless old system.

His sympathies with boys were as true and quick as
those of Frederick Coleman, but his judgment was sounder
as to the degree of liberty that may be wisely allowed a
lad while still a school-boy.

The reforms he introduced were in all respects admirable.

He gave closer attention to the lower "forms"—assigned
a lad to his classes only after careful examination—greatly
extended the scope of instruction—above all, he introduced

a thorough system of order in the routine work of the school. Yet there were but few "rules."

He made it his business as soon as a lad entered, to tell him briefly what he would and would not allow, and there the matter dropped. That he must be truthful and honorable "went without saying." He set his face sternly against the foolish custom of "hazing," and, with all his gentleness of manner, his boys knew that he was not a man to speak twice when it was a question of discipline. He would tolerate no drinking of intoxicating liquors— no card-playing even "for fun"—nor would he allow any visiting between the cottages after nightfall without permission.*

Such were his few "regulations."

His treatment of boys was fair and manly, and his boys, big and little, felt it to be so.

During the session, he himself, even when he had guests, would not touch a glass of wine nor play a game of whist. The "regulations," he held, were for all.

He was a man of amiable disposition and naturally a counsellor of peaceful methods in the settlement of disputes, but, if mediation failed, he was ready, like "Old Fred," to stand by, impartial as a Greek chorus, and see fair play.

As is now the custom of every honorable teacher, he scorned to play the spy, but if a boy was detected violating his well-knowing regulations as to card-playing or drinking, he must leave the school at once.

A second infringement of his regulation about visiting at night, met the same dreaded punishment. No amount of personal or "family influence" could shake his resolution, when he had once decided that a boy must go.

After his marriage, which took place within a few years of his coming to "Hanover," it was his custom, as it was

*Letter of Bishop Thomas U. Dudley.

Arnold's at Lalelam (and to some extent at Rugby) to have the boys often in his house, and to invite them in turn to dine at the family table. His old pupils tell me that his conversation on these occasions was frank to boyishness, and that after dinner he would discuss with them over a cigar whatever momentous question happened for the time to be agitating their little world.

He took long walks with the boys, would constantly drop into their "cabins" for a smoke and a familiar chat, and thus kept himself fully informed as to the state of public opinion in the school.

Outside his favorite classical studies, he was an industrious reader in the field of *belles-lettres*, and constantly stimulated a love of general reading in his pupils. He lent them books—gave freely of his counsel, and still more freely of his money, in the founding of a good school-library, and the establishment of debating societies, and in a hundred other ways made them feel not only the power and sincerity of his own generous enthusiasm for learning, but the strength of his personal interest in themselves, their amusements and ambitions.

Year by year, under his admirable management, the school grew in numbers, until in the years immediately preceding his election to the Latin professoriate in this institution, every vacancy (in his limit of eighty boys) for an ensuing session, was taken before the "long vacation" began. In 1859, after ten years of brilliant success, he was called to the chair of Latin in this University and accepted the position.

It is not my purpose to speak of him as a professor.

His brief tenure of the position forbade the realization of the high hopes, which his friends confidently entertained as to his career on the broader field.

But it is only simple justice to declare that, for the two years he held the professorship, he gave thorough satis-

8

faction to his class, his colleagues and to the Board of Visitors. His powers of acquisition and of concentration were of the first order, as were also his powers of clear and luminous exposition as an instructor.

His reading in the field of the Latin language and its literature was wide and exact, he was fired with a generous ambition to sustain the high traditions of the chair, and, had he lived, there is every reason to believe that he would have left behind him a name in scholarship not unworthy of a place alongside that of his illustrious predecessor. No small evidence of the estimation held of his conduct of the chair, is found in the fact, that, when in 1861 he took the field as captain of a light battery and tendered his resignation, the Board of Visitors refused to accept it and unanimously voted to keep the position open for him. The time was now come when he was to give the supreme proof of how entirely every action of his blameless life was guided by a lofty sense of duty.

To a man of his peaceful temperament and scholarly tastes, military life was in every way repugnant. His life-long ambition had been to make himself a great scholar and, at last, the conditions were all favorable for the full fruition of his aspirations.

Domestic in all his tastes, no blare of trumpet or stirring martial strain ever moved him so deeply as the simple fireside music of a tender voice and the pattering of little feet. But, though "his life was gentle," the elements were

So mix'd in him that Nature might stand up,
And say to all the world, "This was a *man*."

He was a man of deep convictions—he had been bred up in the strict States Rights school, and believed absolutely in the inherent right of a sovereign state to withdraw from the Federal compact.

Like many another at the time, he hoped that temperate counsels might prevail at the last and the Union be preserved, but when Mr. Lincoln, in April of '61, called for 75,000 men to coerce those states, which had but exercised what he held to be their sovereign right, the duty of Virginia seemed plain to him as it did to thousands of others, who, indeed, loved the Union, but who "along with the blood inherited the spirit and the virtues of the old champions of Freedom."

The change wrought in the attitude of the strongest Union men in Virginia by that famous call is familiar to you all. One instance in the case of a fellow student of mine, I recall with amusement.

The majority of the students were strong "secessionists *per se*," as they were then called, and many of us, who had big "tickets" and an unconquerable fondness for billiards, were by no means adverse to "seeking" even "at the cannon's mouth" that "reputation" likely to be denied us in the severe ordeal of the schools. On a sunny morning in April, a knot of us, gathered at "the Blue Cottage," were discussing with great warmth the affairs of the nation. It is needless to say, our voice was "all for war." A friend of mine, then one of the best students in the University, now a grave professor in a theological seminary and who but two years ago refused a bishoprick, alone remonstrated against the abandonment of our studies, and spoke so sensibly and temperately as to cast a very decided damper on our martial aspirations.

Later, during the same day, our young "Sir Galahad," Percival Elliott of Georgia, who now fills a soldier's grave, and myself, walking up to "the Rotunda" from the Post Office, descried hurrying towards us a familiar figure clad in a uniform known to no service in Christendom—a revolver as large as a small howitzer was buckled about his waist and a cavalry sabre of huge dimensions clanked furiously as he came towards us. *Obstipuit visu Aeneas!* We were literally spell bound with amazement. "Why,

Nelson,* what in the name of all that's righteous, is the meaning of this?" "Haven't got time to talk to you, boys— Lincoln has called for 75,000 men—enlisted five minutes ago in 'the Albemarle troop,'" and so sped away our peaceful counsellor of the morning.

Never can I forget the night of the 17th of April, when on the sudden call of the Governor of the State for volunteers to seize the arsenal at Harper's Ferry, the two companies of students enrolled in the University at once offered themselves for the service and made rapid preparation to leave for what we proudly called "the seat of war." As we stood drawn up at the station, awaiting the train that was to bear us away to "fields of glory," Professor Holcombe read to us the official announcement of the secession of the state, and Lewis Coleman came among us to wish us God speed. He scolded us, indeed, in kindly fashion for "running away from our books," but far more eloquent than the "reproof upon his lip" was "the smile in his eye."

Then burst the storm, and, in brief time he felt that, despite his position here, his place was at "the front."

Of his career in the army time forbids me to speak.

He entered the military service as captain of a light battery and rose to be lieutenant-colonel of artillery.

He embraced, indeed, the profession of arms with reluctance, but he discharged the duties of his new position with the same fidelity that had characterized him in the peaceful pursuit of letters.

Everywhere—on the lines of Centreville—on the Peninsula—in front of Richmond—he endured the privations and shared the triumphs of that glorious army to which he belonged. At last on December 13th., 1862, on the historic field of Fredericksburg, came to him the last of

---

*Rev. Kinloch Nelson, D. D., Professor of Greek. etc., in the Episcopal Theological Seminary at Alexandria.

many fights. A few days before the battle, riding with a brother-officer towards Port Royal, he said : "If I am to fall in this war, I should prefer to fall here, for hard by my father lies buried."*

Within three days he received the mortal wound, which won him his last promotion at the hands of the Great Captain.

As the sun came bursting through the mist on that glorious morning, the army from its position looked down upon a scene, which stirred the heart of conscript and veteran alike. Countless batteries, supported by serried masses of infantry, were moving across the plain in all the pride and circumstance of war, sworn to wrest victory from the perch to which she so obstinately clung—the tattered battle-flags of "Rebellion."

Far on the right, as the steady-marching columns passed the River Road, the youthful Paladin, Pelham, his cap bright with ribbons, was seen manœuvring his single "napoleon" within close range of the looming masses of the enemy, doing his *devoir* with a valor so gay and *débonnaire* as drew to him the heart of an army.

As "all day long the noise of battle rolled," Coleman, whose guns were held in reserve near the Hamilton House, sat on his horse chafing at delay, and it was late in the evening when, two guns of Dance's battery being "ordered in" to the left of Poague's "Rockbridge Artillery" on Jackson's extreme right, he sought and obtained leave to accompany the section.

The position was one of the hottest on the whole front. The enemy had got the exact range of the hill on which these batteries were posted, and, opposing thrice as many guns, poured upon them an unceasing rain of shot and shell.

Slowly the sun went down on that hard-fought field and

*Prof. Morris's Sketch of Lewis Coleman in the *University Memorial.*

still our scholar-soldier, calm and serene amidst this fire of hell, cheered on his grimy cannoneers by joyful voice and valiant example.

About dusk in the thickest of the terrific cannonade, he was struck down by a fragment of shell, another piece of which killed instantly an old pupil of his here—a lad of surpassing beauty, who, learned and accomplished beyond his years, gave highest promise of adding still greater lustre to the historic name he bore—Randolph Fairfax, of whom his captain said with trembling lips, when he saw the slight boyish form lying close under the gun he had served so well, the delicately-chiselled features calm in death and the soft brown hair wet with his brave young blood : " Fairfax *looked* more like a woman and *acted* more like a man than any soldier in the battery."

Grievous as was his hurt, Colonel Coleman refused to leave the field, and with an heroic generosity, which irresistibly reminds us of Sidney's self-abnegation at Zutphen, begged the surgeons to attend first to those whose necessities seemed greater than his. Tenderly they bore him next day to "Edgehill" in Caroline, and there, after weeks of intensest agony borne with serene constancy— almost in sight of the old playing-fields of " Concord," where so often his voice had rung out in boyish glee— came at last to the gentle scholar and daring soldier the death counted sweet and honorable.

Of the beauty of his Christian life, there is no need for me to speak. From the days of his eager young manhood, he had sought to rule his every action and utterance by the spirit of his Divine Master, and when he fell on sleep, 'twas not "the iron sleep" of Homeric hero,* slain, even as he, fighting for fatherland, but that blessed sleep, fraught with life eternal, which He giveth His beloved.

*ὣς ὁ μὲν αὖθι πεσὼν κοιμήσατο χάλκεον ὕπνον κ. τ. λ. *Il.* xi. 241.

That briefest and sublimest biography ever penned was his, in truth : " *And Enoch walked with God, and was not, for God took him.*"

Thus, my brothers of the Alumni, I have sought to trace for you the evolution of the Virginia " University School," as it exists to-day, and to portray in homely fashion the lives and methods of the two great school-masters, who were the pioneers of the new education.

But let me not be misunderstood.

It would be doing great injustice to the labors of many excellent teachers to ascribe to the Colemans the whole credit for the improvement in the tone and quality of academic instruction, which marks the quarter of a century between 1835 and 1860. Other schools, some taught by graduates of this University, some by graduates of other institutions, were doing good work, as I can gratefully attest.* But, unquestionably, the Colemans were the pioneers in the great revolution, which within a few years swept away the vicious old order.

To " Concord " is due the inauguration of that glorious " honor-system," which fosters every noble impulse of the boyish heart, and which is to-day the chief glory of our Virginia schools.

To " Concord " and " Hanover " equally, is due the signal advance in the scope and thoroughness of University preparation, which for years gave the young men trained at these schools a prestige here enjoyed by no other students.

And to them again is due that reflex action, which is as truly the distinctive mark of healthy vitality in education as in the human body.

As young men came here with better preparation, the

*I refer to the "Hampton Academy," Hampton, Virginia (Col. John B. Cary, A. M., Principal), where many Virginia lads were fitted for the University.

University steadily raised her standards, and, in turn, her courageous insistance on her tests, compelled a still higher quality of training in the schools.

This has gone on slowly, but surely.

Gessner Harrison, during his latter years here, was wont to declare that pupils were coming to him from the leading preparatory schools with a better knowledge of Latin than twenty years before had been carried away by his graduates.*

Were Lewis Coleman in his chair to-day, he would be the first to admit the same.

Surely to all thoughtful men, who hold dear the higher education in Virginia, it must be apparent that the maintenance of such schools is essential to the security of the high position held by this institution among the great Universities of the land.

They are the natural feeders of the University and must remain so, certainly for many years to come, so long as she maintains her present standards.

When Frederick Coleman began teaching in 1834 there were but 210 students in the University—before Lewis Coleman ceased, there were between six and seven hundred.

In the history of the evolution of every profession, the thoughtful student notes that it grows in honor as it grows in emolument. Such is the history of law, of medicine, even of the church. Not a few men of good social position taught school in Virginia, at least for a time, prior to 1835. Yet the weight of testimony is, that the profession was not regarded, as was the law or medicine, as the profession for a gentleman to choose.†

---

*Rev. John A. Broadus's admirable *Memorial of Gessner Harrison* delivered before the Soc. of the Alumni in 1873.

†As illustrative of this assertion (in support of which I could give numberless citations), Col. Frank Ruffin writes me : " Mr. Thomas Ritchie, who was always an enthusiastic man, had been very much impressed by some of the opinions of William Godwin in his book entitled the *Enquiry*

But when young men of good position saw these two gentlemen of the landed-proprietor class, winning as school-masters such emolument as fell to none save the foremost at the bar or in medicine, great numbers of them felt free to follow their scholarly inclinations, and gladly conse-crated their lives to a calling, which had become in the eyes of the world at once lucrative and honorable.

Such, as I have tried to sketch for you, is "the ever-lasting possession," which these two men bequeathed to Virginia, and surely, in this place beyond all others—here gathered about the feet of our Mother, whom they ever loved with passionate devotion, and who sent them forth equipped for their great work in life—it is meet that we should do honor to their memory and seek to fix their place among our Virginia "Worthies."

When the young Virginian of a hundred years to come shall bend over the page, which chronicles the history of

(*Concerning Political Justice*, &c., 1793), a work which had a great run in its day; and having determined to do that which philanthropy required as his work for mankind, he selected school-teaching as his proper sphere and adhered to it until ill-health compelled him to relinquish it; when he took up what he deemed the next most important calling and became the editor of a newspaper, which he named *The Enquirer* after the title of Godwin's book. When he determined to open his school, which he established at Fredericksburg, his mother (who was my great grand-mother) paid a visit to Judge Roane, her nephew, to induce him to use his influence with her son and persuade him not to follow a profession, which was thought by herself and not a few others of that day to be at best but inglorious and rather beneath the rank and dignity of a gentleman. It is proper to add that Judge Roane had so little sympathy with his aunt's mortification that he sent his son, the late W. H. Roane, to the school. It was from him that I had this account. Though in after life he became very intimate with Mr. Ritchie, yet it was a joke with him to tell him how, when at school, he had sworn in his wrath that, as soon as he got to be a man, he would whip Tom Ritchie for the many floggings he had given him." In its day "*The Enquirer*" was the most powerful paper in this country and it may well be doubted whether any single journal to-day exerts so direct an influence in shaping political measures. This letter of Col. Ruffin rescues from oblivion how it came by its name.

his native state, and shall read with kindling eye and flushing cheek the long roll of those, who have made her "glorious by the pen" and "famous by the sword," though he shall meet there greater names, which, perchance, may quicker stir the pulse's play, yet shall he see there none worthier of his reverence or of his emulation than the names of FREDERICK WILLIAM and LEWIS MINOR COLEMAN.

ADDRESS

AT THE

UNVEILING OF THE STATUE

OF

DANIEL WEBSTER,

NEW YORK, 25 NOVEMBER, 1876.

BY

ROBERT C. WINTHROP.

ADDRESS

AT THE

UNVEILING OF THE STATUE

OF

DANIEL WEBSTER

IN THE CENTRAL PARK, NEW YORK,

25 NOVEMBER, 1876.

BY

ROBERT C. WINTHROP.

BOSTON:
PRESS OF JOHN WILSON AND SON.
1876.

ADDRESS.

I am here, Mr. Mayor, fellow-countrymen and friends, with no purpose of trespassing very long on your attention. I am afraid that I have neither voice nor strength, to-day, for many words in the open air; and I may be obliged to leave for the newspapers much of what I might desire to say.

But, indeed, the Address of this occasion has been made. It has been made by one to whom it was most appropriately assigned, and who had every title and every talent for making it. It was peculiarly fit that this grand gift to your magnificent Park should be acknowledged and welcomed by a citizen of New York, — one of whom you are all justly proud, an eminent advocate and jurist, a distinguished statesman and public speaker, with the laurels of the Centennial Oration at Philadelphia still fresh on his brow. The utterances of this hour might well have ended with him.

But I could not find it in my heart to refuse altogether the repeated and urgent request of your munificent fellow-citizen, Mr. Burnham, that I would be here on the platform with Mr. Evarts and himself, to-day, to witness the unveiling of this noble Statue, and to add a few words in commemoration of him whom it so vividly and so impressively portrays.

Mr. Burnham has done me the honor to call me to his assistance on this occasion, as one who had enjoyed some peculiar opportunities for knowing the illustrious statesman to whose memory he is paying these large and sumptuous honors. And it is true, my friends, that my personal associations with Mr. Webster reach back to a distant day. I recall him as a familiar visitor in the homes of more than one of those with whom I was most nearly connected, when I was but a schoolboy, on his first removal to Boston, in 1817. I recall the deep impressions produced on all who heard him, and communicated to all who did not hear him, by his great efforts in the Constitutional Convention of Massachusetts, and, soon afterwards, by his noble discourse at Plymouth Rock, in 1820. I was myself in the crowd which gazed at him, and listened to him with admiration, when he laid the corner-stone of the Monument on Bunker Hill, in presence of Lafayette, in 1824. I was myself in the throng which hung with rapture on his lips as he pronounced that splendid eulogy on Adams and Jefferson, in Faneuil Hall, in 1826. Entering his office as a Law-Student, in 1828, I was under his personal tuition during three of the busiest and proudest years of his life. From 1840 to 1850 I was associated with him in the Congress of the United States ; and I may be pardoned for not forgetting that it was then my privilege and my pride to succeed him in the Senate, when he was last called into the Cabinet, as Secretary of State, by President Fillmore.

I have thus no excuse, my friends, for not knowing something, for not knowing much, of Daniel Webster. Of those who knew him longer or better than I did, few, certainly, remain among the living ; and I could hardly have reconciled it with what is due to his memory, or with what is due to my own position, if I had refused, — I will not say, to bear testimony to his wonderful powers and his great public services ; for all such testimony would be as superfluous as to bear testimony to the light of the sun in the skies above us, — but if I had declined to give expression to the gratification and delight with which the Sons of New England, and the Sons of Massachusetts and of Boston especially, and I as one of them, cannot fail to regard this most signal commemoration of one, whose name and fame were so long and so peculiarly dear to them.

Neither Mr. Evarts nor I have come here to-day, my friends, to hold up Mr. Webster, — much as we may have admired or loved him, — as one with whom we have always agreed, as one whose course we have uniformly approved, or in whose career we have seen nothing to regret. Our testimony is all the more trustworthy, — my own certainly is, — that we have sometimes differed from him. But we are here to recognize him as one of the greatest men our country has ever produced; as one of the grandest figures in our whole national history; as one who, for intellectual power, had no superior, and hardly an equal, in our own land or in any other land, during his day and generation; as one whose written and spoken words, so fitly embalmed "for a life beyond life" in the six noble volumes edited by Edward Everett, are among the choicest treasures of our language and literature; and, still more and above all, as one who rendered inestimable services to his country, — at one period, vindicating its rights and preserving its peace with foreign nations by the most skilful and masterly diplomacy; at another period, rescuing its Constitution from overthrow, and repelling triumphantly the assaults of nullification and disunion, by overpowering argument and matchless eloquence.

Mr. Webster made many marvellous manifestations of himself in his busy life of threescore years and ten. Convincing arguments in the Courts of Law, brilliant appeals to popular assemblies, triumphant speeches in the Halls of Legislation, magnificent orations and discourses of commemoration or ceremony, — are thickly scattered along his whole career. I rejoice to remember how many of them I have heard from his own lips, and how much inspiration and instruction I have derived from them. To have seen and heard him on one of his field-days, was a privilege which no one will undervalue who ever enjoyed it. There was a power, a breadth, a beauty, a perfection, in some of his efforts, when he was at his best, which distanced all approach, and rendered rivalry ridiculous.

And if the style and tone and temper of our political discussions are to be once more elevated, refined, and purified, — and we all know how much room there is for elevation and refinement, — we must go back for our examples and models at least as far as the days of that great Senatorial Triumvirate, — Clay, Calhoun, and Webster. There were giants in those days ; but none of them forgot that, though "it is excellent to have a giant's strength, it is tyrannous to use it like a giant."

Among those who have been celebrated as orators or public speakers, in our own day or in other days, there have been many diversities of gifts and many diversities of operations. There have been those who were listened to wholly for their intellectual qualities, for the wit or the wisdom, the learning or the philosophy, which characterized their efforts. There have been those whose main attraction was a curious felicity and facility of illustration and description, adorned by the richest gems which could be gathered by historical research or classical study. There have been those to whom the charms of manner and the graces of elocution and the melody of voice were the all-sufficient recommendations to attention and applause. And there have been those who owed their success more to opportunity and occasion, to some stirring theme or some exciting emergency, than to any peculiar attributes of their own. But Webster combined every thing. No thoughts more profound and weighty. No style more terse and telling. No illustrations more vivid and clear-cut. No occasions more august and momentous. No voice more deep and thrilling. No manner more impressive and admirable. No presence so grand and majestic, as his.

That great brain of his, as I have seen it working, whether in public debate or in private converse, seemed to me often like some mighty machine, — always ready for action, and almost always in action, evolving much material from its own resources and researches, and eagerly appropriating and assimilating whatever was brought within its reach, producing and reproducing the richest fabrics with the ease and certainty, the precision and the condensing energy, of a perfect Corliss engine, — such an one as many of us have just seen presiding so magically and so majestically over the Exposition at Philadelphia.

And he put his own crown-stamp on almost every thing he uttered. There was no mistaking one of Webster's great efforts. There is no mistaking them now. They will be distinguished, in all time to come, like pieces of old gold or silver plate, by an unmistakable mint-mark. He knew, like the casters or forgers of yonder Statue, not only how to pour forth burning words and blazing thoughts, but so to blend and fuse and weld together his facts and figures, his illustrations and arguments, his metaphors and subject matter, as to bring them all out at last into one massive and enduring image of his own great mind!

He was by no means wanting in labor and study; and he often anticipated the earliest dawn in his preparations for an immediate effort. I remember how humorously he told me once, that the cocks in his own yard often mistook his morning candle for the break of day, and began to crow lustily as he entered his office, though it were two hours before sunrise. Yet he frequently did wonderful things off-hand; and one might often say of him, in the words of an old poet, —

> " His noble negligences teach
> What others' toils despair to reach." ,

Not in our own land only, Mr. Mayor and fellow-country-men, were the pre-eminent powers of Mr. Webster recognized and appreciated. Brougham, and Lyndhurst, and the late Lord Derby, as I had abundant opportunity of knowing, were no underraters of his intellectual grasp and grandeur. I remember well, too, the casual testimony of a venerable prelate of the English Church, — the late Dr. Harcourt, then Archbishop of York, — who said to me, thirty years ago, in London, "I met your wonderful friend, Mr. Webster, for only five minutes; but in those five minutes I learned more of American institutions, and of the peculiar working of the American Constitution, than in all that I had ever heard or read from any or all other sources."

Of his Discourse on the Second Centennial Anniversary of the Landing of the Pilgrims on Plymouth Rock, John Adams wrote, in acknowledging a copy of it, " Mr. Burke is no longer entitled to the praise of being the most consummate orator of modern times." And, certainly, from the date of that Discourse, he stood second, as an Orator, to no one who spoke the English language. But it is peculiarly and pre-eminently as the Expounder and Defender of the Constitution of the United States, in January, 1830, that he will be remembered and honored as long as that Constitution shall hold a place in the American heart, or a place on the pages of the world's history.

Mr. Webster once said, — and perhaps more than once, — that there was not an article, a section, a clause, a phrase, a word, a syllable, or even a comma, of that Constitution, which he had not studied and pondered in every relation and in every construction of which it was susceptible.

Born at the commencement of the year 1782, at the very moment when the necessity of such an Instrument for preserving our Union, and making us a Nation, was first beginning to be comprehended and felt by the patriots who had achieved our Independence, — just as they had fully discovered the utter insufficiency of the old Confederation, and how mere a rope

of sand it was; born in that very year in which the Legislature
of your own State of New York, under the lead of your gallant
Philip Schuyler, at the prompting of your grand Alexander
Hamilton, was adopting the very first resolutions passed by any
State in favor of such an Instrument, — it might almost be said
that the natal air of the Constitution was his own natal air.
He drank in its spirit with his earliest breath, and seemed born
to comprehend, expound, and defend it. No Roman schoolboy
ever committed to memory the laws of the Twelve Tables more
diligently and thoroughly than did he the Constitution of his
country. He had it by heart in more senses of the words than
one, and every part and particle of it seemed only less precious
and sacred to him than his Bible.

John Adams himself was not more truly the Colossus of Independence in the Continental Congress of 1776, than Daniel
Webster was the Colossus of the Constitution and the Union in
the Federal Congress of 1830.

For other speeches, of other men, it might perhaps be claimed
that they have had the power to inflame and precipitate war, —
foreign war, or civil war. Of Webster's great speech, as a
Senator of Massachusetts, in 1830, — and of that alone, I think,
— it can be said, that it averted and postponed Civil War for a
whole generation. Yes, it repressed the irrepressible conflict
itself for thirty years! And when that dire calamity came
upon us at last, though the voice of the master had so long
been hushed, that speech still supplied the most convincing
arguments and the most inspiring incitements for a resolute
defence of the Union. It is not yet exhausted. There is
argument and inspiration enough in it still, if only they be
heeded, to carry us along, as a United People, at least for
another Century. In that Speech "he still lives;" and lives for
the Constitution and the Union of his Country.

Why, my friends, not even the Dynamite and Rend-rock

and Vulcan powder of your scientific and gallant Newton were
more effective in blasting and shattering your Hell-Gate reef,
and opening the way for the safe navigation of yonder Bay,
than that speech of Webster was in exploding the doctrines of
nullification, and clearing the channel for our Ship of State to
sail on, safely, prosperously, triumphantly, whether in sunshine
or in storm!

Beyond all comparison, it was *the Speech* of our Constitutional
Age. "*Nil simile aut secundum.*" It was James. Madison, of
Virginia, himself, who said of it in a letter at the time: "It
crushes nullification, and must hasten an abandonment of secession." Whatever remained to be done, in the progress of events,
for the repression of menacing designs or of overt acts, was
grandly done by the resolute patriotism and iron will of President Jackson, whose proclamation and policy, to that end, Mr.
Webster sustained with all his might. They were the legiti-
mate conclusions of his own great Argument.

Of other and later efforts of Mr. Webster, I have neither time
nor inclination to speak. There are too many coals still burning
beneath the smouldering embers of some of his more recent controversies, for any one to rake them rashly open on such an occasion as this. I was by no means in full accord with his memorable
7th of March speech, and my views of it to-day are precisely
what he knew they were in 1850. But no differences of opinion
on that day, or on any other day, ever impaired my admiration of
his powers, my confidence in his patriotism, my earnest wishes
for his promotion, nor the full assurance which I felt that he
would administer the Government with perfect integrity, as
well as with consummate ability. What a President he would
have made for a Centennial year! What a tower of strength
he would have been, to our Constitution and our Country, in
all the perplexities and perils through which we have recently
passed, and are still passing! "Oh! for an hour of Dundee"!

No one will pretend that he was free from all infirmities of character and conduct, though they have often been grossly exaggerated. Great temptations proverbially beset the pathway of great powers; and one who can overcome almost every thing else, may sometimes fail of conquering himself. He never assumed to be faultless; and he would have indignantly rebuked any one who assumed it for him. We all know that, while he could master the great questions of National Finance, and was never weary in maintaining the importance of upholding the National Credit, he never cared quite enough about his own finances, or took particular pains to preserve his own personal credit. We all know that he was sometimes impatient of differences, and sometimes arrogant and overbearing towards opponents. His own consciousness of surpassing powers, and the flatteries,—I had almost said, the idolatries,—of innumerable friends, would account for much more of all this than he ever displayed. I have known him in all his moods. I have experienced the pain of his frown, as well as the charms of his favor. And I will acknowledge that I had rather confront him as he is here, to-day, in bronze, than encounter his opposition in the flesh. His antagonism was tremendous. "Safest he who stood aloof." But his better nature always asserted itself in the end. No man or woman or child could be more tender and affectionate.

And there is one element of his character which must never be forgotten. I mean his deep religious faith and trust. I recall the delight with which he often conversed on the Bible. I recall the delight with which he dwelt on that exquisite prayer of one of the old Prophets, repeating it fervently as a model of eloquence and of devotion: "Although the fig-tree shall not blossom, neither shall fruit be in the vines; the labor of the olive shall fail, and the fields shall yield no meat; the flock shall be cut off from the fold, and there shall be no herd in the stalls: yet I will rejoice in the Lord, I will joy in the God of my salvation." I recall his impressive and powerful plea for the Religious Instruction of the Young, in the memorable case of Girard College. I have been with him on the most solemn occasions, in Boston and at Washington, in the midst of the most exciting and painful controversies, kneeling by his side at the table of our common Master, and witnessing the humility and reverence of his worship. And who has forgotten those last words which he ordered to be inscribed, and which are inscribed, on his tombstone at Marshfield:—

" ' Lord, I believe; help Thou mine unbelief.' Philosophical Argument, especially that drawn from the vastness of the universe, in comparison with the apparent insignificance of this globe, has sometimes shaken my reason for the faith which is in me; but my heart has always assured and re-assured me that the Gospel of Jesus Christ must be a Divine Reality. The Sermon on the Mount cannot be a merely human production. This belief enters into the very depth of my conscience. The whole history of man proves it. — DANIEL WEBSTER."

I cannot help wishing that this declaration, in all its original fulness, were engraved on one of the sides of yonder monumental base, in letters which all the world might read. Amid all the perplexities which modern Science, intentionally or unintentionally, is multiplying and magnifying around us, what consolation and strength must ever be found in such an expression of faith from that surpassing intellect!

I congratulate you, my friends, that your Park is to be permanently adorned with this grand figure, and that the inscription on its massive pedestal is to associate it for ever with the great principle of " Union and Liberty, one and inseparable." Nor can I conclude without saying, that, from all I have ever known of Mr. Webster's feelings, nothing could have gratified him so much as that, in this Centennial Year, on this memorable

Anniversary, nearly a quarter of a century after he had gone to
his rest, — when all the partialities and prejudices, all the love
and the hate, which wait upon the career of living public men,
should have grown cold or passed away, — a Statue of himself
should be set up here, within the limits of your magnificent
City, and amid these superb surroundings. Quite apart from
those personal and domestic ties which rendered New York so
dear to him, — of which we have a touching reminder in the
presence of the venerable lady who was so long the sharer of
his name and the ornament of his home, — quite apart from all
such considerations, he would have appreciated such a tribute
as this, I think, above all other posthumous honors.

There was something congenial to him in the grandeur of this
great Commercial Metropolis. He loved, indeed, the hills and
plains of New Hampshire, among which he was born. He delighted in Marshfield and the shores of Plymouth, where he was
buried. He was warmly attached to Boston and the people of
Massachusetts, among whom he had lived so long, and from
whom he had so often received his commissions as their Representative and their Senator in Congress. But in your noble
City, as he said, he recognized "the commercial capital, not
only of the United States, but of the whole continent from the
pole to the South Sea." "The growth of this City," said he,
"and the Constitution of the United States are coevals and con-
temporaries." "New York herself," he exclaimed, "is the
noblest eulogy on the Union of the States." He delighted to
remember that here Washington was first inaugurated as President, and that here had been the abode of Hamilton and John
Jay and Rufus King. And it was at a banquet, given to him,
at your own Niblo's Garden in 1837, and under the inspiration of these associations, that he summed up the whole lesson
of the past and the whole duty of the future, and condensed
them into a sentiment, which has ever since entered into the

circulating medium of true patriotism, like an ingot of gold with the impress of the eagle: "One Country, One Constitution, One Destiny."

Let that motto, still and ever, be the watchword of the hour, and whatever momentary perplexities or perils may environ us, with the blessing of God, no permanent harm can happen to our Republic.

In behalf of my fellow-citizens of New England, I thank Mr. Burnham for this great gift to your Central Park; and I congratulate him on having associated his name with so splendid a tribute to so illustrious a man. A New Englander himself, he long ago decorated one of the chief Cities of his native State with a noble Statue of a venerated father of the Church to which he belongs.* He has now adorned the City of his residence with this grand figure of a pre-eminent American Statesman. He has thus doubly secured for himself the grateful remembrance of all by whom Religion and Patriotism, Churchmanship and Statesmanship, shall be held worthy of commemoration and honor, in all time to come.

---

* A bronze Statue of the Rt. Rev. Thomas Church Brownell, D.D., — for more than forty years the Bishop of Connecticut, and, at his death, in 1865, the presiding Bishop of the Protestant Episcopal Church in the United States, — was presented to Trinity College, Hartford, of which he was the Founder, by his Son-in-law, Mr. Burnham, and was unveiled in the College Grounds, on the 11th of November, 1869.

www.ingramcontent.com/pod-product-compliance
Lightning Source LLC
Chambersburg PA
CBHW032354020726
47499CB00008B/2738